THE BATTLE
AT TITA'S HOUSE
AND OTHER STORIES

DAVID DELGADO

ISBN-10: 171925396X
ISBN-13: 978-1719253963

Artwork by Silverio Hernandez

CONTENTS

David Delgado

PREFACE

The purpose of this collection of short stories is to expose you to reading—to reading anything. Once the habit of reading is formed, you will, of your own accord, become more selective. It's my firm belief that the best way to acclimate yourself to reading is to begin with a short story and work your way upward in both length and complexity, thus letting the myriad and ever-growing vistas of literature open slowly upon you. This allows you to digest and learn to understand themes and ideas without being overwhelmed.

For example, before I read any novels by Ernest Hemingway, I came across his short stories, which caught my attention. After reading his novelette *The Old Man and the Sea*, I became a fan of anything Hemingway wrote, which ultimately led me to his longer works. I had the same experience with Isaac Asimov. In his case I came across a string of short essays that opened my eyes to his science fiction. The point is that I started by reading something, then I graduated to the longer literary works usually, but not necessarily, of the same author. Of course, I would always revert to my first love—the short story.

There is a wide variety of exposure for the reader in this collection. If you are pleased by my surprise endings, let me suggest other authors like Saki, Guy de Maupassant, John Collier, Roald Dahl, and O. Henry. If you enjoy the storytelling, you may read the likes of Jack London, Victor Hugo, Cayetano Coll y Toste, or Arthur Conan Doyle. (Doyle wrote imaginative and exciting short stories aside from his historical novels about his most famous character, Sherlock Holmes.) If, on the other hand, you have an interest in the metaphysical or the occult, you can discover the writing of Edgar Allan Poe, Gabriel Garcia Marquez, H. P. Lovecraft, Carlos Fuentes, or Isabel Allende.

Popular authors of this era are famous and well read for a reason. Agatha Christie, Isaac Asimov, and Stephen King are excellent; they have written works ranging from the short story to the long novel. The idea is to spread out and sample everything: poetry, essays, novels, the Bible, physics, horse-racing scratch sheets, the classics, comic books, scientific journals, wrestling magazines, biographies, science fiction, or mysteries.

These suggestions are only to get you started. Let us get to reading! The more you read, the more selective you get. I trust that ultimately you will reach the short story. If these short works inspire you to seek more stories, my efforts will have been well spent.

David Delgado

ACKNOWLEDGMENTS

I want to acknowledge my family for their part in my work. I am sure they will see themselves in some of the stories. In particular, I want to thank my mom for her hand in leading me safely through life, exposing me to much, and ultimately setting me in the fertile ground necessary for creative writing. My contribution has been an iota of imagination; she will get the credit for the heavy work. I want to gracefully acknowledge those individuals who have been my source of encouragement, always present, always reminding me that the prize goes to the one who finishes the race, not necessarily the swiftest. To those individuals who put me back on course when I deviated, or just plainly stopped, thank you!

INTRODUCTION

Perhaps, seeing this book on a shelf, today's "modern" man may ask what relevance a collection of short stories has in this age of Internet technology.

Dismissing the question without further thought will cheat the prospective reader of a great pleasure. *The Battle at Tita's House and Other Stories* is a thoughtfully sinister collection of writings that will remind the reader that good writing is a pleasure at any age. And often, discovering the story behind the story is equally satisfying.

David Delgado began his writing career in 1984 with *Mrs. Winfield's Business*, which he entered in the fifth annual Miami News Halloween Scary Story Contest. Of 5,000 entries, Delgado received an honorable mention. *Obsessed With the Obvious* was written in the fall of 1993, when the Mont Blanc Writing Instrument Company, together with the department store Neiman Marcus, held a murder mystery short story contest to celebrate the issuing of Mont Blanc's limited edition writing pen called the "Agatha Christie." The pen featured the 1920's Mont Blanc design of an intricately engraved sterling silver snake with genuine ruby eyes. The contest required submissions to include the words Mont Blanc, sterling silver, Neiman Marcus, snake, Agatha Christie, ruby eyes, fountain pen, and the word "Meisterbutten." (I don't know the meaning of the word "Meisterbutten" and don't believe the author did either! Incidentally, the author ultimately acquired an Agatha Christie snake-clipped fountain pen, but he did not win it in the contest.)

Delgado is of Puerto Rican descent, and though he was born in New York City, he spent much of his childhood on the island. As a result, many of his stories have a Latin flavor. Anyone who was raised in any Latin American country or visited relatives back home can relate to *The Telegram Man* or *Dinner with Grandma*.

Delgado also seems to enjoy the macabre and is fascinated with the supernatural. *The Battle at Tita's House* transports us to the exotic island of Puerto Rico where power and spirituality form an uneasy mix. This story was originally penned as an entry to a short story contest sponsored by the Encyclopedia Britannica. The theme of the contest was the seven deadly sins of excess. The author focuses here on the deadly sins of envy and pride, embodied in people who are presumably less prone to committing sin: a Protestant reverend afflicted with pride and a humble healing lady afflicted with envy. We see these two sinful forces embrace in a demonic contest stemming from two geometrically opposed holy sources.

Delgado draws on his vast legal experience as a judge in the Circuit Court of Cook County in Chicago, Illinois. *Saving Grace* was written for the Chicago Lawyer Magazine Short Story Contest and was first published in August of 1993. It portrays a grandmotherly-type character whose solution to evil is, at best, contrary to her saintly appearance. This story was intended as a play on the paradox of a servant working for two masters, which is a problem commonly addressed in the field of agency law.

In *State vs. Bloom* and *Obsessed with the Obvious*, Delgado addresses racial and ethnic stereotypes, prejudices, and bigotry. *The Telegram Man* is a story of love, losses, and hope. It is an accumulation of human traits put to a boil until they reach a crescendo of anxiety. Social justice tangents are taken only to return the reader to the story with a jolt. *A Debt Collected* develops the age-old theme of selling the soul to the Devil for a price and suggests that a person's soul is lost the moment one tries to change his identity. If you are ashamed of your ethnicity and cut away your ethnic roots, death results, even if it is in a limited sense.

The Five Gold Krugerrands was inspired by a true event in the late 1980's in Fox Lake, Illinois when Salvation Army volunteers discovered that someone had mysteriously deposited five gold Krugerrands from the Republic of South Africa in the donation bucket. There was no publicity around the discovery, but later, at a Christmas celebration, a comment was made about the Krugerrands and was overheard by a reporter, who wrote a story that was placed on the AP wire. The mysterious appearance of gold coins into a Salvation Army donation bucket has now become a tradition, and every year someone in the Chicago area drops a gold coin, whether it is a South African gold Krugerrand, a Canadian gold Maple Leaf, or a Mexican gold Peso. Delgado shares that this is his favorite short story. It is a story that starts simply but becomes quite intense when philosophical thoughts about man's existence and man's purpose in life are explored. Then we are rewarded with a wonderful ending. For certain, Delgado's endings are rarely predictable, leaving readers intrigued, troubled, and more importantly, questioning.

In some cases, a day in the "Delgado Universe" can seem at first to be rather mundane as he draws on everyday people and common events to weave a lay person's tale. However, as the reader continues, he may notice a subtle menace creeping beside him. Perhaps, just perhaps, all is not as it seems. Or is it? It is this ability to lead the reader from stability through perplexity, to confusion, to shock, that makes these stories a success.

The Renaissance Man again hints at his legal background, but he takes a turn and challenges readers with his extensive liberal arts, classical education—no doubt from his studies at the University of Puerto Rico or from his days teaching philosophy at the Benedictine Monastery Abadía de San Antonio Abad in Humacao, Puerto Rico.

It is this classical education, imparted through his writings, that makes his stories popular teaching materials. I am pleased to have joined the ranks of educators who have used his stories as a teaching resource. Other schools where his stories have been used include St. Augustine College, Loyola University, Amherst College, Wright College, John Marshall Law School, Quincy University, and Chicago State University.

Patricia A. Rangel, MA, JD

Professor of English/Communications

Wright College, Chicago, Illinois

1 The Telegram Man

There were dark clouds on the horizon, threatening the August heat, when we first heard about the telegram man. I had been playing with the guys, but at the moment we were lying on our backs, conserving energy, just watching the sky and waiting for the clouds to bring relief.

News of the telegram man's arrival swept over the group, entangled with a new wave of heat. Something had happened. We were looking at each other, distinctly aware than an additional stillness in the afternoon had been created. The birds, the wind, the leaves all seemed to be holding their breath after the telegram man was mentioned. A swell of anxiety was beginning to foul tita air.

"What? What?"

The telegram man was coming all right. He had parked his car as far up the road as he could and was now making his way down the path that started where the tar-paved road ended.

Victor had seen him first and had heard the neighbors give the telegram man directions to Mrs. Mina's house. It was Victor's voice we heard from the dirt path. Victor had taken off to notify every household along the way of the pending development. You could see every house he entered wake up in activity. It was only proper that Victor was the one spreading the news, as he was the fastest runner of all the eleven-years-olds in the neighborhood. Victor had come up to where we were resting and yelled the news at us.

"There's a telegram for Mrs. Mina and the telegram man is on his way!"

Victor's mom was going to be mad at him. He was still in his Sunday School clothes and staying clean was impossible for him. I wondered if notifying the neighbors would justify getting his clothes dirty. His white shirt was already soiled in the front and his left short sleeve had a dirty palm print where someone may have grabbed him to slow him down. When I looked at his shoes I was certain; Victor was going to get a whipping.

"Did you ever wonder why the telegram man's pouch is smaller than the bag used by the regular mailman?" asked Jimmy. "It's so he can make a fast get-away! These guys always bring bad news!" We all laughed the contagious laugh that Jimmy started. "Things are not always the way they seem. The size of the bags could be misleading. The smaller the bag, the greater the grief and evil they bring."

Jimmy was thirteen-years-old, but part of our school group. Jimmy knew everything. He should have been in the seventh grade, but the teachers had held him back. "The teacher don't like me," Jimmy would say. I believed him. Jimmy knew so much more than the rest of us. He always had an answer for the world's questions. Where does bad luck come from? How does hair grow? Why do Catholics have to eat fish on Fridays? He just happened to know the means to satisfy the curious among us. Unfortunately, he couldn't please the teachers.

Today he was educating us on the telegram man. "They are exactly like the postman, except for the size of their bag. And check out the cap. The telegram man will be wearing the type that policemen wear. It's to remind us that they have more authority than those who deliver ordinary mail." Jimmy was full of information as we cut through the bushes to make a shortcut run to Mrs. Mina's house.

Victor was taking the long way, spreading the announcement, a self-proclaimed Paul Revere. I could see that the back of his shirt was also dirty. Yep, Victor was going to get it.

The telegram man turned the bend down by the creek. He would now have to trek up the hill in the sun all the way to Mrs. Mina's house. This was my first glimpse of a live telegram man. I was disappointed. I had envisioned an energetic, crisply-pressed young fellow with a square cap, like the ones in the movies, guys who stand at attention with a hand outstretched, asking for a tip after making a delivery.

This was an older man, round at the belly. His yellow and black uniform did not fit right. His uniform looked too tight and it was wet with sweat. Across his body he had the pouch. It was a thin leather pouch just like Jimmy had predicted.

The delivery man was being escorted by Paco and Lucas. These boys were in the fourth grade. They knew where Mrs. Mina lived. The delivery man was now assured to reach his destination. I couldn't help but think that Victor should have been the one to escort him. That service would have saved Victor his whipping.

The fat man was laboring up the hill, his face dripping with sweat. His walrus mustache looked too big for his face. He looked at the sun and then toward the horizon. The threatening dark clouds were not advancing. At the moment he would not be getting cloud cover. He stopped momentarily to wipe his face with an oversized handkerchief. He could see the house. He was in no hurry. He would catch his breath, then attack the hill once more.

The curious, who had been following at a distance, were now shamelessly catching up. It occurred to me that maybe the telegram man was purposely pausing. If this were true, then this man was creating drama. What kind of human being would take a job like this? This soulless character had undoubtedly choreographed this dance before, I was sure of it. What I was not sure of was the reason for the telegram. And why to Mrs. Mina?

"It's because all her kids are in New York and that is where telegrams come from," Jimmy said. "All telegrams come from New York and they go straight to mothers. It's a risk mothers take for allowing their kids to go to the United States. Sooner or later Mrs. Mina was bound to get one."

I felt a rush of guilt. I love my mom, yet I had already thought about going off to New York. To think that someday I would cause the commotion that would trigger a telegram to be delivered to my mother. You see, one of the greatest goals for young people of our barrio was to immigrate to the United States. The young people talked about going abroad to the United States as young people today talk about going off to college. It was the expected thing to do as soon as you were of age. What else was there? To congregate by the shades of the mango trees waiting for the return of the most adventurous with their glorious stories of life in New York? No sir! The desire was to join the ranks of the valiant ones, those who would charge into the unknown, then return full of trinkets, presents, and stories.

Oh, those tales from the North! Tales that would cement us around the storytellers' feet waiting to hear the minutest detail of their adventures. This would be an adventure that would be lived time and time again as a cousin or neighbor would take charge at the dinner table. And after completing his story, another cousin would add the exploits of his journeys. The storytelling would ultimately spill unto the patio—more wonderful accounts of what to expect when you went across the ocean to the United States. It is a marvelous thing what a young body can endure and the adolescent mind can magnify.

What was seldom shared was any hardship that existed, like the piercing cold that comes when winter surprises the ignorant from the Caribbean who have only a sweater to call a coat. "Things are not always as they seem," is what the Reverend McCarthy would say, especially to the young adults. "You cannot always go by the rosy accounts as told by those rare lucky ones." This message the reverend would preach and the older folk would second. "The first problem you face is that of language. New York is not waiting for you in Spanish. The Americans speak only English." Here the reverend would exaggerate his accent. "And what about the cold? Have you considered what to do when the temperature drops to snowing and you don't have warm clothing?"

Sometimes we had negative accounts which, by the way, did not prove to be less entertaining, like the time Luis' suitcase was stolen at the airport in New York. He claimed he only took his eyes off the luggage for "a few seconds." He had to wear the same clothing for a month. Or the time Clara spent the night sleeping in the subway with the winos. She had made it to an address, in the middle of the night, that turned out to be the "front" of a building. The back of the building was gone; it had burned down.

Negative stories were not the favorites, but once this particular ribbon of taboo was broken, other bad experiences would also be told, stories of avarice and greed, stories about jealousy among peers and evil deeds among their own kind. The atmosphere would get somber and heavy, especially if there was an account of a loved one's death.

No matter! As always, the evening would end with the teller of tales counting the days until the next crop of immigrant workers would be shipped to the asparagus-picking fields of New Jersey or the sewing machine sweatshops of the Lower East Side of Manhattan. So did the adolescents who were yearning for the day when they could follow the steps of those who had preceded them in the odyssey to the North.

It was in adjacent rooms that the elders would congregate. This group understood the preaching of Father McCarthy. They had felt the loss of the company and affection of their loved ones. They understood the coldness of people fashionably described as "minding their own business." How could they explain the loss of the fellowship of their own kind? Or the taste of bigotry, and malice, and injustices? Or that special sense of despair and hopelessness in a foreign land that can only be felt by the soul of wisdom?

To those promises of opportunities Mrs. Mina had "lost" her four sons and one daughter. "Lost" was the term used by Mrs. Mina herself, since the siblings, having migrated, had not been back to visit. The last to migrate was her daughter Maria. The four sons did not write much. That was the task entrusted to Maria. The men's job was to watch over Maria and to stay out of harm's way. Maria in turn was the contact for Mrs. Mina and her source of news from the mainland about her family. Maria, in the beginning, was faithful to her task, but then the letters sent back home were less frequent. She did continue to write, but ultimately her communication was just like the other daughters lost to the northern colossal.

Of the sons "lost" to the metropolis, Manuel had caused Mina the most suffering. It was said that Manuel was the tallest, most handsome, smartest, and most ambitious of her crop. Still, he was the son who had questioned the existence of God one Sunday morning, to the eternal embarrassment of Mrs. Mina.

"This boy will come to a bad end," was Father McCarthy's prediction.

Before migrating, Manuel had grown a beard, the type of beard that the vagabonds and communists wear. Mrs. Mina was heartbroken. Then it got worse.

From the United States the news arrived that Manuel had married a white woman. She may have been German, a heretic for sure. Few details were known. He never asked for Mrs. Mina's blessing for the marriage. The bride never met his mother. That was the final act of disrespect. After that report, Mrs. Mina had insisted that Manuel's name never be mentioned in her house again.

Word traveled fast. By the time the boys got to Mrs. Mina's house, Mrs. Victoria was making a dash across the patio to her best friend's house. Mrs. Blanca was already with her best friend in the kitchen. This house had large rooms and little furniture, giving the impression that the rooms were larger than they really were.

Mrs. Mina's children were all grown and gone; she had the house to herself. Now that there was less activity and less furniture, all that was left was a memory of what once was a hub of activity. More than once she had contemplated leaving such a large house, but what if one of the children came back to live with her? Where would she put them? She had opted to stay. She would grow old on mere hopes and memories. The girl, once grown, would go to live with her husband. The boys, once gone, would only be back to be buried.

The three women were in the kitchen, an adjacent room connected to the house. They were not saying anything to each other. These three widows would hold their ground at the end of the house until the telegram man got there. Blanca and Victoria were standing guard, carefully stroking Mrs. Mina's dress sleeves. Their minds were racing with speculations of countless tragedies, yet they said nothing, talking only with their eyes, awaiting the inevitable arrival of the unwelcome visitor.

The telegram man made his way past the few onlookers who had gathered in front of the house. He went up the five steps leading to the porch and gently rapped on the open door. The entourage stayed waiting outside, looking in through the open windows.

"Excuse me, good afternoon," he said. "Telegram for Mrs. Guillermina Luisa Lopez Contreras," he said, a little louder. He stressed the word Mrs., as he knew was expected.

The three snapped to attention as if caught by surprise. They walked in unison, like three soldiers, toward the front of the house. It was as if the Devil himself had accompanied the telegram man. The heat in the house was suffocating. Mrs. Blanca felt her knees would buckle. She was going to faint. She tightened her hold around Mrs. Mina's arm to support herself.

Jimmy was correct, the telegram pouch was thin. It contained only the envelope with the telegram for Mrs. Mina. The envelope was extended to Mrs. Mina, who stood in the middle of the three.

Mrs. Mina hesitated. It was Mrs. Victoria who snatched the telegram from the outstretched hand. Of the three, Victoria was the only one who knew how to read.

The telegram man tipped his hat and said, "Good day ladies." This man was a veteran! Without turning around, he backed out the way he had come and, taking advantage of the momentary stillness that filled the room, he made his exit before the envelope was opened. Jimmy was right again; the lightness of his load made his escape easier.

Victoria slowly examined the black and yellow envelope. The heat was unbearable. There was no breeze blowing. There was stillness in the crowd. No one was breathing. A lady of Mrs. Mina's generation had started to pray the rosary. At the far end of the house, two other elderly women were already consoling each other, quietly sobbing.

Mrs. Victoria was now satisfied that the envelope's seal was intact. She viewed the little wax paper window of the envelope and acknowledged, with a faint nod, its address: "to Mrs. Guillermina Luisa Lopez Contreras."

At this instant, Mrs. Mina felt a rush of love from her friends. Her eyes were cloudy with tears, but she could "see" with her heart how her friend vacillated. She could sense that Mrs. Victoria was procrastinating, trying her best to shield her friend from the inevitable.

She was blessed with good friends. Mrs. Mina felt fortunate. In the stillness of the heat, she felt she could float on her blessings. She had grown old with good friends. Her eyes looked down and focused on the envelope and the petite, bony hands that were holding it. The hands were trembling. Mrs. Mina substituted her shallow breathing for deeper breaths.

Mrs. Victoria, as if on cue, stopped her hesitancy. She flipped the envelope, broke the seal, and pulled out the folded telegram. The household held its breath. The onlookers kept silent. Those who were praying or sobbing lowered their voices. She read the telegram to herself and then smiled. She kissed Mrs. Mina in relief and then hugged her. The telegram had less than fifteen words that read as follows:

God Bless Mother. Stop. You are now a grandmother. Stop. Twins girls. Guillermina and Luisa. Stop. Your Manuel.

Mrs. Victoria and Guillermina Luisa were holding each other, still crying. In a corner, some old man was fanning Mrs. Blanca, who had finally collapsed on a chair. The household was breathing again. Outside by the bushes Victor's mom had Victor by the hair and was scolding him the old fashioned way. She had already slapped him a couple of times for getting his clothes dirty.

"What did I tell you?" Jimmy asked as he put his arms around Carlos and me. "Things are not always the way they seem. Let's go. This drama is over. If we hurry, we can catch up to the delivery man. Let me tell you about the cars that telegrams are delivered in..."

We began running along the hill, trying to catch up with the funny little man who delivers telegrams.

2 Mrs. Winfield's Business

What I most clearly remember about this case was the court appearance of Mrs. Winfield. That tall, slender, elderly woman was actually arguing jurisprudence. She seemed to know more about law than the appointed public defender.

My mind was elsewhere then. In my daydream I was planning my upcoming vacation. Not much to plan, if you thought about it. We always go to Michigan in the fall, attend a football game, yell like banshees, and battle the first frost and the hay fever symptoms. My whole family gets hay fever! We then buy pumpkins for Jack-o'-lanterns and we are back home before Halloween.

The judge and prosecutors were amused but not impressed with Mrs. Winfield's arguments. The judge's patience was finally brought to an end when this elderly lady told the state's prosecutor to "shut up" and called the public defender a mongoloid idiot. She got twelve months probation, with the special condition that she see the social work unit of the P.D.'s office. That's how I got involved in this case. I'm a social worker with the Dade County Public Defender's Office.

I already mentioned I was absorbed by my daydream throughout the proceedings. When the judge called my name to give me the case, that's when I really woke up. I couldn't believe it—a new case on my last day before vacation! No need to panic, at least not yet.

It was only 10:00 a.m. The sheriff would bring her down to my office before lunch, and I would work through lunch. Working through lunch would be my excuse to leave early. Leaving early on Friday is the common practice anyway. I would not be missed; a perfect plan.

I did not receive word about Mrs. Winfield until almost 2:00 p.m., and only because I was pressing the jailhouse. She had apparently gotten loud with the sheriffs, protesting her innocence, blaming it all on the mischievous doings of a certain fellow named "Wheelo." The sheriffs didn't buy any of her stories and had decided to let her cool down in the lockup when she starting demanding her immediate release.

Even though I had found her, she would not be released without her file. This is not unusual, as the file would contain a copy of the court order releasing her from the custody of the county sheriff. How do you lose a senior citizen? What incompetence!

Her file had somehow fallen into the hands of a jail custodian, a rookie on the job who didn't know what he was doing, or what to do with the files. I found it odd that he didn't know the simple in-house procedures of the lockup. He had succeeded in not only losing the old lady but also losing the file. Plus I didn't like the rookie's grin. This fellow just came across like he was purposely trying to hide the file. Hey, slow down, be careful about blaming others, I told myself; this is just another government employee acting normal.

I was beginning to think there was some conspiracy to ruin my vacation. I tried to instill some sense of urgency by flapping my arms around and shouting. This whole incompetent scenario had just cost me at least four hours head start of my valuable vacation time. I finally got some attention. A deputy sheriff supervisor promised to have Mrs. Winfield in my office within ten minutes. Mrs. Winfield was quickly becoming a very famous person.

She arrived under protest, again demanding her immediate release. I knew then I had a winner. She finally became calmed and apologetic, mentioning that fellow 'Wheelo' she had previously talked about in her morning court hearing and in the lockup, and how 'Wheelo' was behind this whole misunderstanding.

"Always interfering with my business. Wheelo is an evil man," she said, her eyes and forehead quite intense. "He will use the craft to cover his abusive ways. That's his plan. I am not fooled."

"Use the what?" I asked.

"You know...the craft. I am of the Old Religion," she said.

My mind was made up. I was going to place her in some social service program over the weekend and by Monday she'd be a state Family Service Department problem. I, of course, would be fishing somewhere in Michigan.

She was very eloquent during my interview with her. She gave me a home address in Hialeah for a house she claimed she owned. For a moment I thought of all my "Santeria" clients and then I dropped these thoughts.

"The house is all paid up," she said. One of her sons, Edward the doctor, had gotten the house for her. I proceeded to get Edward the doctor's office phone number, her sister's telephone number, and other information as the intake forms dictated. I was in a bit of a rush; the part on religion I skipped. That part is optional anyway.

The interview went smoothly. Everything was in order—or so I thought. She had a place to stay. She didn't seem to present any imminent danger to herself or society. I could even send her home. But I didn't. I had that indescribable sense that told me something was not right. Yes, everything seemed in order, but it did not feel right. It's the social worker feeling we social workers sometimes get. It's like our sixth sense. That's how we end up as social workers in the first place, at least those of us who have answered the true calling.

How could the senses take precedence over logic? Especially right before my hard earned vacation! I never got a clue that this case, of all my cases, would be notorious.

My years of experience kept telling me something was not right, but I was going to let her go. Yes, by that time I was rushing. I could send her home. That was the least paperwork. But I was not going to let this grandma go home alone. Not at that hour, not in downtown Miami. It was that feeling again.

Over Mrs. Winfield's polite protests, I attempted to telephone her sister. What came on the telephone line was an operator's recording informing me that the sister's telephone number was not in service. I realized that her son's office telephone number had a Broward County extension number and that it was quite improbable that she could live on Pink Flamingo Road in Hialeah.

I confronted her with my concerns about the conflicting bits of information, especially the apparently blatant lie about her sister's current telephone number.

"Oh, never you mind, young man," she said, waving me off. "I just talked to my sister and told her to come and pick me up here." A few seconds later she started laughing and gesturing as if she was in fact communicating with her sister. "As a matter of fact," she said, addressing me now with a straight face, "she'll be here in about ten minutes."

I was beginning to think that I was not being taken seriously when she added that she communicated "often" via mental telepathy.

I paused, took a deep breath, and stared at her. The disbelieving look that I gave Mrs. Winfield forced her to explain.

"You are probably of the school that stands on the proposition that the only way to transmit a thought to another person is through a recognized channel of sensation," Mrs. Winfield continued.

"What?" This old lady is unbelievable, I thought.

"You know what I mean," she added. "You don't believe that a mind can communicate with another mind. This would violate all existing laws of physics. Then again, a quantum physicist would quickly recognize that a nuclear particle does communicate with other particles in keeping orbital harmony. This is done contrary to modern laws of physics, or any viable means of communication." Then she leaned over and in a whisper stated, "The scientists can't explain the translocation of these nuclear particles either."

"Huh?"

"Come on, you know what I mean—translocation. Modern science can't explain how a nuclear particle moves from one orbital sphere to another orbital sphere. These particles appear to move more by magic than by any established law of motion. Don't worry son," she said as she gently tapped my shoulder, "the scientific community will know when I am ready to explain it to them."

That did it! That confirmed my initial gut feelings. I should have sent her to the funny farm the first minute I saw her. I could kick myself. Now I had a real problem. Where was I going to find a social service agency I could commit her to after 5:00 p.m. on Friday? Remember, I'm dealing with governmental employees that turn into pumpkins by 2:00 p.m. on Fridays.

I frantically began searching for an agency to take her off my hands. I found an old friend who owed me at the Community Mental Health Clinic and he agreed to take her. I called the cab company that does our livery and rushed Mrs. Winfield out of the building. The cab was waiting. I wrote the address of the clinic on the back of my card, gave it to the cabbie, and then all hell broke loose.

"Wheelo!" Her scream chilled my bones. Anger and determination overcame her. "I'm not getting into that taxi with him! Wheelo has already caused me enough grief. He's really gone too far. I have a mind to send him back to his master Lucifer this instance."

The cabbie was grinning but looked as confused as I felt. I was getting that social worker feeling again. Had I seen this man before? I tried to place the face and the grin.

Keep it moving Buster. You have a vacation to attend, I told myself. I was also feeling embarrassed because of Mrs. Winfield's outbursts.

At that moment, another cab pulled up. Great! It was one of our regulars. This time I pushed her in. The cab driver knew where the mental health clinic was, and Mrs. Winfield went peacefully.

I didn't get a chance to apologize to that 'Wheelo' fellow in the first cab. He was gone by the time I finished with Mrs. Winfield. I had not even noticed he had left. What a day! It had been a hectic and frantic day. I needed the vacation.

I had a wonderful time in Michigan. I had problems with my

sinuses (terrible hayfever) but I handled the fever well. We came back with a couple of pumpkins, which the kids carved into impressive Jack-o'-lanterns.

When I got back to the office I had some visitors. They were ransacking my things, looking through the drawers and filing cabinet and not being neat about it. I would have thrown them out but my boss was with them and seemed to be approving.

"These boys are with homicide," my boss said when he sensed I expected an explanation. "They are looking for information on one of your clients. Give them a hand." Then he left me to the mess and the two gorillas.

"You better come with us. We're going to the morgue. The stiff should be finished with his autopsy by now. Show him the victim's picture, Frank." The smaller of the two was giving the orders.

Frank was surprisingly polite. He did not make me feel guilty for not being able to identify the victim. The picture of this victim's face was difficult to make out. It appeared as if someone was grabbing the person's head by his hair and was holding the head backwards. In addition, the skin from both sides of the head was being tightly stretched backwards, exposing all of this victim's lower teeth. In short, the deceased did not look like any one of my clients.

I don't like looking at dead bodies. I never have. The face in the photo I had not been able to place. The body at the morgue, however, I recognized immediately.

It was Wheelo!

"The strangest case I've ever seen, Sarge," said the old man in the white smock. "This is off the record, boys. On this one I am at a loss. There is no evidence showing an outside entry into the chest cavity to pull the heart out. Of this I'm completely positive. It appears that his heart was pushed out of his rib cage from the inside out! All this trauma, and without damaging the heart! The heart was then punished further. As you can see, it's really bruised. The large vein leading to the heart was severely pinched, which ultimately caused his death. The whole affair must have been mighty painful. Look at the frozen tightness of the neck muscles. This shows that his last act in life must have been a piercing cry of terror! This one is really strange, really very strange. Where do you boys get 'em?"

They were now all looking at me. I told the detectives and the doctor all I knew about Wheelo, and I tried to explain how I might have seen him at the county lockup dressed as a deputy sheriff, how Wheelo looked a lot like the rookie who lost the court files. I explained for the fifth time how my card could have gotten into Wheelo's wallet. I had innocently written the address for the transport of Mrs. Winfield to the health clinic on the back of my card and given it to Wheelo when he was driving the taxicab.

I talked about my job, my days in court, all I knew about Mrs. Winfield, and my vacation in Michigan. I just kept my mouth moving, talking without breathing. I was really nervous as we sped toward the mental health clinic.

The director himself greeted us. Yes, Mrs. Winfield had stayed at the clinic. And yes, the fellow in the picture Frank showed him had been seen at the institution three or four days ago, "during visiting hours." Wheelo had caused quite a disturbance. Actually, Mrs. Winfield had caused the entire disturbance. She had become hysterical, claiming loudly that this fellow had "interfered with her business once too often." She wanted to send him to hell and meant it.

"For the good of all my patients I personally escorted this man out of the building. Then, two night's ago, Mrs. Winfield decided to leave and of course she was forcibly detained. You can't blame the day shift for her escape," continued the director. "They weren't aware of the previous night's incident. It seems she impersonated a lab technician, entered the hospital "G" wing, worked all morning in the labs, and then left at lunch. She fooled everybody. She's an expert in this field! You can ask any of my lab personnel. I was told she waited for her sister and yes, an older looking lady did pick her up in front.

"How Mrs. Winfield contacted her sister is still a mystery. Outside communications with a patient are strictly prohibited. Even the phone calls that are allowed are closely monitored. We don't want our work undone by the insensitive chattering of third parties. A lot of progress is lost by the good intentions of friends and family members.

As a matter of fact, the only telephone that exists on her floor is at the nurses' station. We checked the log since she was admitted; there have been no unauthorized calls. It's amazing. Mrs. Winfield just walked out the front door at noon and there was her sister, waiting.

"I have explained all of this before, to the other policemen, when we reported her missing." The director was now sounding concerned. "You know this is not like we are running a maximum security prison here. These whackos should be sent to real hospitals!" For the director, the interview was over. Cursing under his breath, he was gone to his more pressing problems.

"I do believe we have a real slick one here, Sarge," said Frank. "Now we really have to find her and ask her a few questions."

Frank turned and addressed me as we all headed toward the car. "What business did you say Mrs. Winfield was in? Is she a witch or what?"

I didn't answer; I was asking myself the same question.

3 Obsessed With The Obvious

It was a gruesome death. The victim was a young woman, maybe twenty-three years old. Her throat had been sliced from ear to ear. The trachea had been cut open and the internal tissues spilled out. The reality of the matter was that it looked pretty awful. There were signs of struggle and blood all over the attic apartment.

The body of the female victim had been discovered by a factory co-worker named Luba, who had come at approximately 5:30 a.m. to pick her up. It's the unwritten understanding in the carpool that there is no waiting. You have to be out in front of the house at a certain time for pickup, no excuses. The victim had never missed a day of work; she had never been late. Luba found her friend's absence unusual. Luba decided to investigate and wake her up, if needed.

Luba went to the back of the house and up the back porch steps that led to the attic apartment. Going up the steps, Luba noticed the blood. She then noticed the schoolbooks scattered by the entrance door. She found the door ajar, stepped into the house, and discovered the fruits of the crime.

The apparent perpetrator had been found just down the alley inside a garbage bin. He also was covered with blood and had his throat cut open, an apparently self-inflicted wound. This all added up to a bloody mess and it wasn't even 8:00 a.m.

Sergeant Stanley Stefanski sat in his squad car, brooding. He could only think of the detective that headquarters had assigned to assist him in the investigation of this crime. It was that Puerto Rican lieutenant who was interning with the department. Earlier in the morning, he had received, via the radio dispatch, the news about the Puerto Rican being assigned to his detail. Stefanski was beginning to feel miserable. He was sure the worst was yet to come.

Stan could not place the reason for the resentment, but he could feel it creeping through his body. He wanted to blame the Puerto Rican but he knew the Puerto Rican was not the cause of his problem. The real problem was the way he was being treated by the higher ups in the department. The Puerto Rican would be treated well and tolerated for a few months and then he would be gone. Back to his island! Stan would continue in the fraternity of his department and in the ridicule that he felt certain was going on behind his back.

Stan could feel he wasn't being treated right by the department. In this case, he had gotten the assignment almost three hours after the discovery of the bodies. Already the Violent Crimes Division had sent to the scene a team of investigators, *real* detectives, to investigate the crime. These investigators had dropped by with a crew of lab technicians, photographers, and the works. Now, three hours later, after the prima donna detectives of violent crimes had come and gone, after they had made their grand entrances, stirred around everything that could be stirred, and ultimately determined that this was an "open and shut" case, they called headquarters to send a subordinate to wrap things up.

When headquarters called you to "wrap things up" this really meant that your presence was for public relation purposes. You were required to ask questions, talk to relatives, and fill out inventory forms and questionnaires—grunt work. The investigation was, for all practical purposes, done and concluded. It was like going to a wedding after the cake had been cut, served, and eaten.

Stan's displeasure intensified as he became aware that all he was doing was waiting, waiting for a cop who was not even a real member of the department. God only knows why this foreigner had been sent here to the States in the first place. Maybe teaming up with the Puerto Rican was just another way of furthering his punishment. Today was just another set back. He was a full sergeant but it seemed he would never make detective class.

"Detective class" is the unofficial rank a police officer gets when he is called into the Violent Crimes Division. Stan had the seniority, had passed the detective exam, and had been given detective salary, but he was still doing dustpan duty, still being the brunt of the Polish jokes, still not being white enough.

The only way he could move up in class was by conducting some meaningful investigation and by solving some crime. Stan recognized that, at the rate he was going, he would be passed over. At that very moment, instead of chasing clues at some other crime scene, he was here doing the menial jobs, which any raw recruit could competently accomplish. Worse, he had practically finished interviewing the last family member and he was still waiting for the Puerto Rican. He wondered if this Latino was always late.

Stan did not see Luis Ortiz arrive. Luis Ortiz was ushered to Stan's squad car by one of the uniformed police officers on duty. Stan's first impression of the Puerto Rican was that he smiled a lot.

"Lieutenant Ortiz, sir, at your service," said Ortiz, stretching his hand out in greeting.

"Lieutenant in what, the Puerto Rican army?" replied Stan, without bothering to shake his hand. "Where have you been? Here in the United States we get to work on time. This crime was discovered at about 5:30 a.m. this morning. You were waiting to get here for lunch maybe?"

"I apologize, Sergeant Stefanski." The grin on the Puerto Rican's face had not diminished.

Stan cut Ortiz off with a wave of his hand. In any event, he was in charge of this "wrap up" and it would be done effectively and quickly. "Are you in the homicide division back home, Mr. Ortiz?" Stan had decided not to call him lieutenant or detective.

"No, no, I'm not, Sergeant Stefanski," replied Ortiz.

The response reinforced Stan's suspicions of the Puerto Rican. This guy probably couldn't even write in English. He couldn't help me even if there was something to do, Stan thought. Also, the Puerto Rican looked too well dressed for Stan's taste. This Ortiz fellow had probably gotten his suit in some Italian suit surplus store. The suit was nicely tailored and made Ortiz look sharp. Great! Stan thought, another Latino show-off hotdog. Another Latino who lacks any sense of urgency. Stan felt all the more that he had been singled out for punishment by the department. Stan concluded that he did not like Italians, nor their suits, nor any Puerto Rican living outside of his Caribbean island. Especially one with a smile carved in concrete.

"You can go back to wherever you came from, Ortiz. The work here is done," said Stefanski. Stefanski was feeling really clever. "There won't be much learning for you in this case. It's an open and shut case. A classic example of murder-suicide."

Ortiz did not leave. He continued to observe Sergeant Stefanski conduct the questioning of Ivan, the last family member to be questioned in the matter.

Ivan was a big fellow, a rookie in the County Sheriff Department, currently in the last stages of his training. Ivan looked clean and his uniform was well pressed. He had left the job this morning immediately upon learning of the homicide to be close to his family.

Ivan essentially corroborated the story of the other family members. The previous evening he had dropped the whole family off at the movies. At approximately 6:00 p.m. he ate supper with his brother William at a neighborhood restaurant. He took his brother William to his house and returned to pick the family up at the movies. Everyone was in the house before 11:00 p.m. No one had seen or heard anything, nor was there any suspicion that a crime had been committed upstairs in the attic apartment.

The coroner established the time of death at approximately 9:00 p.m. That is why no one heard the noises of the tremendous struggle that had taken place upstairs. Had someone been in the house, the noises would have been easily heard.

Ortiz observed Ivan's brother William against the adjacent house wall. He was a bit younger than Ivan, but also a big fellow. His arms were crossed defiantly and Ortiz could see the bulging muscles. The tattooed snake with ruby eyes that he had tattooed on his arm looked bigger and more menacing than the snake his brother Ivan had tattooed on his arm.

An old lady approached the interviewing squad car. She was carrying a tray with coffee, cups, milk, and a sugar bowl. She was dressed in black, already observing a period of mourning, as was probably the custom of her native Poland.

"You gentlemen are welcome to cake or cookies in the house if you like," she said with a heavy accent. She then turned and walked back into the house.

No one had spoken in the presence of the dignified lady, with the exception of Ortiz, who said thank you. This woman most definitely made her presence felt.

"You still here, Ortiz?" barked Stefanski.

"Yes sir, Sergeant. I was assigned by your headquarters to assist you in this investigation of the murder. Double murder, I may add," said Ortiz.

"I know what headquarters did, and I already told you, it's an open and shut case. The Mexican killed the girl. He then sliced his own throat open and tried to crawl into that garbage bin in order to spill his guts out. We found the Mexican boy lying on top of the garbage bags next to the Meisterbutten beer cans." Stefanski pointed to a large garbage bin three garage doors south of the house.

"You mean Meisterbrew beer cans," corrected Ortiz. "As you are incorrect in this observation, you are also incorrect in other assumptions, Sergeant Stefanski." Ortiz was talking directly at the sergeant without blinking.

"You think this is a double murder, wise guy?" The sergeant was being loud and defensive. This Puerto Rican hotdog is trying to show me up in front of my men, he was thinking. "What other assumptions am I miserably mistaken in?" he continued sarcastically.

"To begin, you are assuming that I am late. On the contrary. I started on the case before you even arrived here. I have also been to the morgue and have inspected the two corpses. That 'Mexican fellow' which you mentioned did not cut his own throat in an attempted suicide, as you suspect. First of all, the young man was not Mexican and secondly, he did not commit suicide, he was murdered. Murdered by the same person who killed the girl.

"I don't believe this incident started out to be a double murder," continued Ortiz. "The killer in his haste did the best he could under the circumstances and made it out to look like a murder-suicide. The murder could have been more efficient by puncturing the young man's throat, but instead he went to the trouble of slicing his throat from left to right. This was made so that it would look like a suicide. The murderer was wrong, however. A left to right suicide wound assumes a right-handed perpetrator. Our victim was left-handed. Furthermore, a self-inflicted wound would have started higher in the neck. If self-inflicted, the wound would have been directed obliquely downward and would have been deepest at the beginning and shallow toward the end. This boy's wound is low, deep, and even. The neck wound could not have been self-inflicted; this act was done by someone else. Someone with big arms, I would add.

"We can assume that as soon as the investigators from your Violent Crime Division fully digest these facts, they will be back. Your headquarters will probably remove you from this case, which will further add fuel to your present state of discontent. I suggest that instead of directing any further hostilities toward me, you devote your energies to the proper investigation of this murder."

The Puerto Rican was right about the boys in Violent Crimes. If what Ortiz was saying was true, they would definitely be back.

"Now you're the one making the assumptions, Mr. Ortiz. Assumptions about hostilities," said Sargeant Stefanski, very much on the defensive now. "I'm not being hostile toward anybody."

"My apologies then, Sergeant; please accept them. I guess I misunderstood your gestures; for instance, your waving your hand in my face, sending me on my way. Your failure to shake my hand in greeting when we first met. Thinking I would not be able to assist you in this investigation because I don't investigate homicides back home. Castigating me for being late, a most misguided belief. And lastly, you proved your ignorance when you tried to ridicule me for being a lieutenant in the Puerto Rican army. You should know that the Commonwealth of Puerto Rico is a political entity somewhat similar to the Commonwealth of Massachusetts in that it has no army. I am a lieutenant in the police force of Puerto Rico. I'm in the division that deals with terrorist and counteracting terrorism, and I do my job well.

"You don't have to be tough to do a job well," continued Ortiz. "You could do a lot to correct your image by refraining from engaging in grotesque acts. Eliminate stirring your coffee with your expensive Mont Blanc pen, for instance. That could be a big positive first step. Do you have any idea how ridiculous you would look if that fountain pen started leaking in your coffee?"

The sergeant was stunned and speechless by the rapid-fire talk of Ortiz and, acknowledging the good points made by his colleague, he burst into a contagious laughter that soon spread to those within hearing distance. Stefanski was beginning to view the Puerto Rican in a different light. *A fresh set of eyes may be what I need to help me out,* he thought. For a moment Stefanski thought about saying something friendly, then quickly decided against it.

"Maybe we can start anew, Sergeant Stefanski," continued Ortiz. "I suspected a murder when I first arrived here this morning. I found it odd that the young man had traveled the distance from this house to the garbage bin, bleeding to death, and, despite his exhaustion, had found the strength to jump into the bin.

"Unfortunately, the detective team from Violent Crimes had their own assessment of this situation and my comments were of little value. You see, Sergeant Stefanski, your detective team was obsessed with the obvious. That's when I decided to accompany the corpse to the morgue. I wanted to verify my own suspicions. What we must do now is find the murderer. I lay no claim to being the world's greatest detective," said Ortiz with a grin. "That title is already taken—penned by Agatha Christie, and claimed by that now famous Belgian detective. I am still considered very good at my job. I'm not a genius, just gifted at figuring out what is more likely than not and then following my intuition. In this life you can never be positively sure. I just try to be close. You should try that technique. It works in the field of solving crimes.

"You will find that my training in capturing terrorists is somewhat similar to yours in capturing criminals. We are both basically doing the same thing: chasing the perpetrator of a criminal act. We are both hunters!

"A crime committed because of a passion for a cause is not to be confused with a crime of passion. These crimes are of two different species. In a crime of violence, the criminal is a different type of prey. You're dealing with a human being that has no conscience or is just plain bent on evil. With patience, proper deductions, and detective work, you will catch your man. The violent criminal is an easy prey.

"On the other hand, a person who has a conscience, who sincerely believes in a cause and now commits crimes in furthering that cause, is a harder prey to catch. Even if the perpetrator's logic is warped, what you have is a soul with a passion who has resorted to criminal behavior in order to further his positions. It is within this circle of criminals that you will find the terrorist and the savvy fanatical. You will find the frustrated who will not hesitate to become a martyr. Here you will find very intelligent individuals, a much harder individual to capture than your typical vandal bent on an occasional murder. You will find that the easier prey to catch is your common hoodlum."

"How did you figure our Mexican was left-handed?" asked the sergeant.

"I didn't figure it out," Ortiz replied. "I asked his mother and I asked his brothers. And by the way, the young man and his family are from Venezuela, not Mexico. I asked for and checked his baseball glove. The young fellow was left-handed, believe me. He lived just across the alley, about four houses north of this house. That's the reason I arrived here through the alley. I was retracing the possible route the young man took last night before he was murdered.

"I trust no one has been allowed into the apartment," Ortiz added.

"No one except the crime lab and the detectives." Stan was now cognizant that the lieutenant was taking command. "This whole back of the house and the alley has been roped off. We also have uniformed policeman posted."

"Sergeant, continue your interview with Mr. Jaworski. I'll be right back. I'm going to take up the coffee and cake invitation," said Ortiz.

After a brief period, Ortiz returned, folding his notepad and pocketing his pencil. The old lady in black was accompanying him. Upon reaching Sergeant Stefanski, Ortiz began saying, "Allow me to reconstruct what actually happened, or at least what more than likely happened. Ivan Jaworski did take the family to the movies and did go to dinner with his brother William. After dropping William off at home, Ivan returned to his house, but not to his first floor dwelling. He went upstairs to the attic apartment to see his cousin and to continue with his romantic advances. She was not alone. She had just returned home from her night school classes with the young man who is now dead. I can assume Ivan felt a vested right in demanding the young lady's affection because of the attention and investment he had made in her.

"He had assisted financially in getting her here from Poland. Ivan's mother tells me that Ivan paid for the plane ticket and helped her get her current job at the factory. This assistance among family members is not uncommon. Hispanics do it all the time.

"Ivan is also the one probably responsible for the expensive gifts of gold and sterling silver which I noticed in her apartment. It appears that she was grateful for the gifts. She couldn't have afforded them on her own. She even saved the Neiman Marcus shopping bags, but obviously she was not grateful enough. She refused Ivan's advances and then a struggle ensued. It got violent. Why the use of the kitchen knife is a question I can't answer, but the knife was used on her throat.

"The murder of the young man was quite unfortunate. According to the young man's mother, he had returned from the night school, where he studied English as a second language. Yes, these two victims were both attending night school together. Yes, the victims knew each other and maybe this is the friendship that Ivan wanted to disrupt.

"The young man walked the girl home, then went to his own house without noticing that he had kept her books. Upon discovering that he had her books, he returned to the attic apartment and came upon a murder being committed. That is why the books are all over the porch. He could have escaped, but the gallant lad came to her aid and was overpowered by Ivan, who was the stronger.

"The young fellow also put up a good fight, got his throat cut, but did not die right away. Mortally wounded, he fled the apartment, chased by our killer. They didn't get far, because the young man collapsed and died. It was easy at that point for Ivan to drag and dump the body in the first garbage bin that would accommodate the corpse. Note that the young man had no reason to go south in the alley. He lived just a couple of houses north of this apartment. This fact seemed to me most unusual indeed. This murder was at the last moment tailored to look like a murder-suicide. The knife has been found in the apartment, but I'm sure that no fingerprints will be found on the handle."

Turning to Ivan, Ortiz continued, "Now that I have a plausible theory and a viable suspect, how do I prove that Ivan committed this crime? Since there has been a tremendous spillage of blood, we will follow the trail of blood. I notice you have a fresh uniform on. I'm told that you had a freshly pressed uniform on last night also. I believe you committed the crime before you changed your clothes last night.

"Your mother tells me that you own three full uniforms. She also takes great pride in you being a member of a law enforcement agency. She insists and takes pleasure in washing and pressing your uniforms. It's a common phenomenon among proud mothers. My mother did the same with my uniforms.

"Mr. Jaworski, one set is hanging neatly pressed in your closet, you are wearing a uniform now, and one set cannot be accounted for. Your mother and I have looked for it everywhere and we just can't find it. By the way, I didn't need a search warrant, because I was invited into the house by your mom for cake and coffee."

The old lady, who had been listening attentively, walked up to her son and slapped his face in disgust. She was clenching her fist and shaking with anger. She knew he had done it; she was crying before she turned around to head back into the house.

"A lost bloody uniform?" The question by Ivan was hardly audible.

"Now what is really going to do you in is your shoes," continued Ortiz. "Leather is a porous material and will retain traces of blood. If you were in fact in that apartment, the shoes will prove it. If the shoes were soiled with blood, it's possible that traces of blood will be found in your automobile and in your room. I'm going to have to inspect all your shoes, including the ones you have on. I have been told that those shoes on your feet are the ones you had on last night. For the inspection of your shoes and the inspection of the car and house I have already requested the necessary warrants.

"You understand that I must insist that you put these handcuffs on," said Ortiz, looking into Jaworski's eyes. "You are under arrest. Please Mr. Jaworski, you know how it's done."

Immediately, the uniformed police officers were upon Jaworski, cuffing and placing him under arrest. Turning to Sergeant Stefanski, Ortiz ordered that the Miranda warning be recited to Ivan.

"I'll be leaving now, sergeant. In reality, it's been a pleasure to have made an additional friend. The search warrants will reflect that these documents were ordered by you as lead inspector of this investigation." Both men were now smiling, Ortiz with a smile of satisfaction, Stefanski with a smile of disbelief and bewilderment.

"If there is nothing further, sergeant, I beg to be excused," said Ortiz. Ortiz was going to stretch out his hand in a farewell gesture and then stopped, remembering Stefanski's earlier lack of manners. Ortiz would wait for the sergeant to make the first move.

The sergeant did think about the handshake for a moment, then decided against any demonstration of friendship or gratitude. He reasoned that an outstretched hand would be an admission of equals or of his earlier errors—or worse, a sign of weakness. The idea of a hand shake was again dismissed.

"Yes, Lieutenant Ortiz, you are excused," was all the sergeant said.

4 Renaissance Man

Professor Joshua Benjamin sat up, out of his body, as he had done six times in the past. Out-of-body experiences are not as uncommon as you would think. They are just difficult to control or consciously create. If Joshua had learned one thing in all his parapsychology studies, it was that anxiety was sure to bring one on.

Joshua was a professor of law, the College of Law representative in the university Senate. That afternoon he had been intellectually humiliated at the hands of Professor Matarri on the university Senate floor.

Joshua had seen this happen in the past—a floor debate gone personal, ultimately ending in a one-on-one battle of wits. To the winner the laurels of victory; to the loser the branding scarlet stigma that would ruin a life in the academic community.

He never thought it could happen to him. He loved knowledge; he was a Renaissance man, learned scholar, a master exposed to many disciplines: law, mathematics, philosophy, medicine, the physical, and the metaphysical.

In addition, he was a stout man, a man of presence, commander of respect. The birthmark, a la Mikhail Gorbachev, that adorned his forehead was not a disfiguring curse; it was a sign, a seal to identify him, to set him aside from the common mortal, to identify him for great things.

The burden of that afternoon's defeat, together with the fact that Helena was dying, produced an accumulation of fears and anxieties that Joshua had never before confronted.

Yes, his beloved wife Helena was dying. She was going through the high fever, which the doctors had predicted would come at the end of the end.

The events of that grim day, coupled with the medical warning buried deep in his subconscious, were triggering anxious reactions within his being. An unconscious fertile environment was being created for an out-of-body experience to happen. Above all, he didn't want his Helena to die. A raw will to prevent the inevitable was being added to the existing combinations of happenings. Joshua knew death was imminent. He had to act now! And in this cloud of mystic confusion, in this edge of the twilight of a dream, he willed his inner being to be lifted. During the night, the out-of-body phenomenon happened.

Joshua contemplated the listless body of what was once his Helen of Troy. The glows and colors of life that are easily noticeable in this dimension were fading from her. Joshua was correct in his assessment. Helena would not last the night amongst the living.

Joshua felt himself float toward the ceiling and, for the first time, was conscious of the fact that he felt no fear. On his first experience, his heart had practically stopped from fright. Over the past years, because of acquired understanding, the fears, though diminished, still remained present. Today, he had no fears. He had a purpose. He knew he could not stop time, but maybe he could prevent death.

The Goddess of Death appeared from nowhere, then stopped. A bone hand held the hourglass with cryptic writing that spelled a name. The labeled name was alien but Joshua knew the glass belonged to Helena. The sands of the funnel were almost gone. Death stood motionless, at a distance, awaiting the drop of the final grain of life, the signal for the moment to snatch the soul from her living body.

Joshua had always pictured Death as a man. He now knew Death was a woman. Her features were shielded from view by her black hooded toga, but he sensed the features of a woman. Death's amber eyes glowed in the depths of the grayish background and somehow Joshua detected a lazy grin.

Quietus knew why Joshua was there. Her macabre eyes were grinning in amusement. To think that a puny mortal could impede the inevitability of time.

Joshua was not fazed. He was a man on a mission, out to champion the cause of his Dulcinea.

Death's attention shifted to the up-held hourglass. The moment was fast approaching. Death drifted toward Helena, the hourglass held high, the grains almost zero.

How do I stop this apocalyptic beast? Joshua thought. There was determination on his part. He would embrace her, maybe grab the hourglass. He had to impede her movements! To delay would prove fatal. He would attack Death now!

Joshua wanted to move toward the invader. His body, however, merely drifted and did not respond to this command. What do I do now? thought Joshua, and while he pondered this question, Death brushed past him.

The Psalmist was right—there is a time for everything under the heavens, even death. Death's proper timing in Helena's case had been interrupted so that Death could not complete her mission. The brush against Joshua's left side had been the slightest, but it had been a disruption nonetheless. Ending a life at an improper time would disrupt a greater harmony. Death conceded the moment. She contemplated Joshua, acknowledging that a soul had eluded her grasp. As Death retreated, Joshua could detect new sands in Helena's hourglass.

Death would return, this Joshua knew, but for the moment, he had won. The victory was his. He could rejoice, he had beaten Death, he had saved his Helena, and he had conquered the world of the non-living. What an accomplishment! His place among the history of educated men was now assured. He knew of no case where Death's quest had been foiled. The methodology of what he had done was not clear, but the results spoke for themselves. He had blocked Death's progress. Aristotle, the father of all Renaissance men, could not top this. Joshua could join the ranks of Pico de la Mirandola, Da Vinci, Bacon, Newton, and still his feat would not be outdone.

He secretly planned how he would orchestrate future trips into this world of the undead. Not having to worry about Helena, he would concentrate on knowledge. He would become the legal scholar of legal scholars. He would crush that imbecile Matarri and then go on to conquer the law schools of the East. Joshua felt lust for power and position.

Helena's recovery, although not total, was in fact miraculous. The doctors were at a loss to explain the reversal in Helena's condition.

In this world of shadows, where there is no anguish or laments, where a worry is alien, Joshua had felt no pain, a mere drain on his left side when Death had brushed past him with her vestments.

Joshua's ailment was quickly diagnosed. The electroencephalogram test results showed extensive damage to the brain. The subsequent brain scans just confirmed the results. Joshua had suffered a massive cerebral hemorrhage. Joshua was oblivious to these facts. He never would perceive that his wife was now the worried one, that there had been a loss of his vitality, his health.

It was not readily apparent to Joshua how long he had been in this melted world where Dali's flaming giraffes ran wild. He longed to return to his Helena, the law school, to quash his nemesis Professor Matarri...

As he pondered how long he had been absent from the real world, Quietus once again appeared at a distance. She stopped, then came at him at instant speed. Then stopped. Joshua acknowledged her presence by faintly nodding. His mind raced through thousands of thoughts. With no reason or design, his thoughts rested on a John Donne quote: *Now, this bell tolling softly for another, says to me, Thou must die.* Josh smiled to himself; he recognized that the quote had been placed in his mind conveniently by Death.

Death held her familiar hourglass, raised as a beacon, an hourglass with little sands left, with letters spelling a name: Joshua. Joshua was not surprised to read that the hourglass belonged to him.

A sense of fear poured over him as Death seemed to float directly in front of him. He could detect movements in Death's vestment, yet he could detect no wind. All Joshua could feel were the cold tentacles of fear's embrace.

Oh God, was he scared! The orange-yellow eyes projected a burning fright. Cold chills of fear sprang from his chest and then raced up his neck. Still, Joshua resisted. He would not allow this flourishing wall of terror the opportunity to cloud his senses.

Again Joshua became keenly aware of his surroundings. He recognized that he was an alien in a lost dimension between light and shadows, where anything and everything could be known, but where at present he somehow found himself lost in ignorance. Immobilized, he watched the hourglass. His fright increased as his life sand dwindled.

In all his wisdom and newfound knowledge, Joshua discovered himself at a lost as to how to act. He knew what he had to do. He had to run, to get out, leave via the cowardly route, and return to his familiar world!

It was useless; his body would not respond to his commands. He knew nothing about movement in this dimension. The simple act of returning to his original state had turned into a monumental task.

Joshua willed his being to wake up, but he felt paralyzed. He was trapped. There were no sounds in his screams of fright. Joshua longed to stretch his arms, to rip the bubble of this twilight world. He felt exhausted. He was losing this battle. A form of terrible panic that can only be perceived in this state of existence was quickly overcoming his senses.

As Death came nearer, Joshua's torture intensified. There was nothing left of the once courageous Renaissance man. The will to resist the embrace of Death was rapidly evaporating into nothingness. He needed a little time; that's all he needed.

Death edged closer. Joshua now knew the secrets that had eluded alchemists throughout history—the transmutation of elements, the preparation of a philosopher's stone. Preparing an elixir of life potion to extend this moment would be child's play. All I need is a little thread of time, he thought. He had so much to share! How was it possible that Death was coming for him now?

Now he knew the truth about justice and the answers to the mysteries and wonders of the world. Now he knew the answers to the riddles that had stumped the wise throughout time. Now he knew the location of Atlantis, the conspirators in Kennedy's assassination, the reasons for the disappearance of Democritus' books, and the numerical value of infinity. He now had facts and answers about the Ark of the Covenant, the truth behind Luis Alvarez's theory on the demise of the dinosaurs. He had answers!

He had to get back. There was unfinished business with Professor Mattari. He had to avenge his public humiliation. He had his Helena to return to. He needed to show her the secrets of long lost treasures. He now possessed the tools. He needed time, just a little...more...time.

Joshua fixed his attention on Death. He could see that his sands were almost zero. He furiously sought the courage he once had. He could, indeed he would, make a stand as he once had done.

On the mark, Death sprang toward Joshua, her skeletal teeth grinning, the empty hourglass held high in one hand, the bony fingers of her other hand reaching for his face like a talon of a rabid bird of prey. Death's fingers pierced his forehead and in a moment of white heat all that was to be known became known.

And at that point the living Joshua ceased to exist.

5 Saving Grace

Willie Stone woke to another day of torment. His demon, his wretched companion, was up on his conscience again. It seemed that, lately, the companionship of this malignant force had been constant.

What did the Bible say? *When an evil spirit comes out of a man, it goes through arid places seeking rest and does not find it. Then it says, "I will return to the house I left." When it arrives, it finds the house swept clean and put in order. Then it goes and takes with it seven other spirits more wicked than itself, and they go in and live there. And the final condition of that man is worse than the first."* *(Matthew 12:43)*

Will I steal or rob again today? Will my sins be forgiven? Willie contemplated his mom, a God-fearing woman. This quest for evil was not her influence. For the past twenty years she had done her part in committing him in the ways of the Lord.

Willie reached back in his memory. He could see himself being dressed by his mother, being taken to church, a routine which would be followed every Sunday and sometimes during the week. He would go to the Mt. Sinai Holy Rock Methodist/Baptist Church where his uncle was the pastor. This was a small storefront church that would stay small. Membership, including children, had never peaked thirty. (Willie had more than once wondered if this could be God's way of telling them all to wrap it up and join a larger church.)

His faithful attendance ceased when he starting going to the community college. Then Willie became smarter than the reverend. His questions became sharper, his debate crisper. He ultimately traded the fellowship of the Holy Rock Church for his college community. And then he traded academia for the hustle and sins of the streets.

Grandma was in her bedroom, on her knees by the bed. Her moments of private prayers had turned into marathon prayer sessions. Grandma made no bones about interceding for Willie. She had seen him part from the way of the Lord and this fact was breaking her heart.

"All your accumulative church time will not save you from eternal damnation. You must remain faithful to the Lord. You are backsliding! Change your ways or for sure Satan will snatch your soul," Grandma would tell him.

The thought of Satan taking his soul kept creeping into his consciousness. What a horrible thought—seeing Lucifer face to face! What about the stronger power of God? Hadn't God saved him once? If God is the most powerful, wasn't Willie now saved for all eternity?

Thinking a moment, he realized that he had repented many times. How many demons now possess me? he thought. He grabbed both his ears, then his face, and with these thoughts he left the house. He had to leave. There was too much praying going on. The spirits of evil within him were being disturbed. He marched toward the subway. He would rob today as he had done before.

He stepped into the nearly empty subway car. Seated across the aisle he saw an older Hispanic lady, an easy prey judging by her scrawny frame, wrinkled face, and thin gray hair pulled back into a bun. He would take her by the neck, punch her puny face against the window, stomp her if needed, and take her purse.

He quickened his pace toward her. She wasn't moving. Was it defiance or terror on her part? His eyes met hers. Was it confidence?

She had noticed him from the moment he walked in. It had to be divine providence that he would step into her car. This was a lost soul bent on doing wrong. She had noticed him, yes, but she had felt him before she had seen him coming.

For more than four decades she had been a faithful servant of God. She thought of herself as having the gift of discernment, a fact she had corroborated numerous times. And now she had a revelation that this boy was not only deep in sin, but also could be saved.

"Are you saved?" she asked, the question sounding more like a command. Her outstretched finger stopped Willie on the spot. Her eyes were piercing. Her air one of confidence. She had no fear. The angels of the Lord were sitting next to her. Of that she had no doubt.

Willie felt a chill for an instant. He felt he had to be cautious. His demon companions were telling him to be careful with this feeble old lady. Was it the Bible she clutched in her hand? Did she have a gun? Or the unthinkable—was she a servant of God, a person he could not harm? Could she be under the command of a thousand angels? The Bible says that the angels of the Lord protect his servants.

The chill surrounding him increased as he pondered in what circle of hell he would fit for attacking one of God's anointed. Would his hand wither or stay stiff if he reached for her? Would God strike him dead? What about God's mercy?

"You need Jesus, son." She spoke softer now. "Sit down, please." She turned her knees toward the aisle so he could slide past her to her right and sit next to the window.

Yes, that's what he needed. To sit down. He was choking. His breathing was fast and shallow. His throat was dry. His heart was pounding. The demons inside him were trembling in the presence of this holy woman. There was no doubt that this woman had that super power that comes from prayer. How many hours a day did this woman dedicate to worship and prayer? It had to be many. Just like the many demons he now possessed.

The chill he now felt was one of death. He imagined legions of demons in his being. They were stealing his reason. He felt faint. He decided he would not harm her. With these thoughts he started to feel better. He would not contest the power of God.

His relief was short-lived as the old lady began conversing with him. He had not been listening; he was just trying to calm his heart, anxious for the subway to make its next stop. He could not catch his thoughts in this woman's presence. He had to get out.

"Are you saved?" She was speaking sweetly.

How would he answer? He had given his life to Jesus many times, but many times he had parted from His ways. His thoughts went back to getting away from this woman, getting out of the subway.

"Escape!" his legion told him. "Get up and escape!" He was, however, paralyzed.

"Repent!" she said. "You have a troubled soul. God will forgive you. I sense you have people praying for you. Is that true?"

The question jolted him. How did she know? This woman was truly a woman of God. There would be no use in lying. He nodded as he said, "Yes."

"I'm Sister Grace. Let me pray for you, son. Do you want me to pray for you?"

"Yes," he said as he nodded again, bowing his head in prayer. He no longer desired to escape. He wanted to be saved. The subway stopped and took on a teenage couple that procured the furthest seats in the car. Willie noticed nothing. He was deep in prayer. His body quivered. He was seeking salvation. His demons were battling. This was war! He would triumph over his devils. He would be strong. He felt level-headed; relief was coming. The murmurs of Sister Grace's prayers were distant. The swaying of the train added to his intoxication. Pounds of guilt and frustration evaporated from his spirit. He could feel his soul being cleansed as he silently asked God for forgiveness.

"Will God forgive me again?" Willie asked without raising his head.

"You will receive forgiveness as long as the request is sincere," Sister Grace answered.

Yes, his request was sincere. He wanted to be good. He wanted to spend eternity in heaven.

"Yes, I want the Lord in my heart." And, at that moment, tears flooded from his closed eyes. The powerful shoulders again quivered. Sister Grace sensed his repentance. She turned slightly toward him, her left arm draped casually across her lap and the purse that was wedged between them. She stretched her right arm across the back of the seat, gently caressing the back of his head before gripping his neck firmly.

His body stiffened as his wet eyes winced. The dagger first penetrated the rib cage. It then effortlessly pierced his heart.

For an eternal instant pain engulfed his body. The pain's tentacles gripped his chest. They squeezed; the breath of life was leaving his body.

Willie knew he was dying. In that moment of desperation he wanted to reach his side to remove the invader to his body. His arms would not respond. His brain had decided that stillness would be the best remedy. There would be no movement for fear of worsening the condition. His last efforts were to open his eyes, to see his assailant. His eyelids, however, would not open. His body slumped to rest against the window.

Sister Grace contemplated her handiwork and felt satisfied. She had succeeded again in snatching another soul from the grasps of the Prince of Evil himself. There was no doubt in her mind that Willie crossed her path so that she could intervene in the rescue of his soul. The only sure way to guarantee his salvation was to eliminate the possibility of his returning to sin.

She had felt his weakness and confusion just as she had sensed his repentance. He would sin no more.

Her body shielding her motions from view, Sister Grace withdrew the dagger and gently replaced it in her purse. The dagger slid to the bottom and came to rest on the crusted blood from her previous assaults.

6 A Debt Collected

The courtroom was full. It was another lucrative case for Lou Salby. His associates were doing the preliminaries but soon he would take over and put on the show that the spectators were expecting.

Right in the middle of the trial, the metamorphosis started. It started as a simple tingling at the heart. The tingling crept down Lou Salby's left side, reaching his left thigh, where it increased in intensity. Then the itching came. The itching started right behind the knee and then went down his side to his ankle. Salby caught himself scratching. He stopped. He was wrinkling his imported tailored suit.

That's when he caught a glimpse of the Devil. There he was, no pitchfork, horns, or goatee. The stranger had slipped behind the judge and clerks and was strolling toward his table as if no one could notice him.

The intruder was impeccably dressed. He was wearing the same clothing Lou had on, a pastel green suit, white turtleneck sweater, tan loafers with socks, and a diamond studded bracelet. He was coming for

Salby.

"What did you expect, Luigi Salvatore? I'm Luzbel, angel of light. You didn't really believe I'd appear wearing red and breathing fire. How many people would I convert looking like that?"

From behind Luzbel, a demon shyly appeared. He was a short creature, half goat, half man, very much like Pan, the Greek god of pastures, forests, and flocks.

"In his image you will become when you enter into my service, Luigi Salvatore," said Satan, pointing at the creature and stressing the last vowels of both names with a grin that deformed his face.

Lou Salby had not heard the name of Luigi Salvatore in over thirty years. That was his birth name. That was the name that had once been his shame. He had left that name behind when he left his native land. How can an immigrant prosper with a name like 'Saving Something'?

Lou finally spoke. "You can't be real."

"Oh yes, we're real, and only you have the privilege of seeing us," replied Satan. There was no expression, just a statement of fact. "You know why I'm here?"

"You are here because of that silly pact!"

"A most serious covenant, which you sealed with your real name. Done while you were still loyal to your kind, in the prime of your wisdom, in those days when you had less, but you had more," replied Satan with a laugh.

Luigi remembered giving up his Christian names as partial consideration. A name was of little consequence. It was his soul that was the real prize. He realized now that by giving up his name he had inadvertently begun to do away with his identity. In a way, the transmutation of his inner being had commenced back then.

"You must remember the pact you wrote in Latin, using looking-glass letters," continued Satan. "You wrote it from right to left, according to tradition. The contract in which you sought confirmation, in a sabot in Toulouse. You were satisfied then, back when you summoned Astaroth, Beelzebub, Elemi, and Leviathan. When you trapped them all in the triangles you drew on the ground, you saw them take form from the smoke you provided with the candles at the base of each triangle. You have fame, success, fortune. You have the gift. Look around you and see how people have flocked into this courtroom to see you. Besides, there is not one request that I haven't complied with. Today I came to claim your soul, Luigi Salvatore!"

"But...but I'm not dead yet," protested Luigi. "You have to wait until my death."

"When I can claim your soul is not specified in the contract. The very contract that you wrote. Where does it say that I have to wait for your death? I've more than fully complied with my end of our agreement."

Again, the Devil was correct. Luigi was the author and knew the contract. When he had to perform was never addressed. On this issue, the contract was silent. He had assumed that it would be some time immediately after his death.

"By chance, you were not thinking of cheating me out of what is due to me, were you counselor?" the Devil inquired as he came closer. There were no expressions, just the questions.

Yes, Luigi had thought about not fulfilling his part of the bargain. In the days of his youth, during the poverty and struggles as a novice attorney, his commitments were heartfelt. It was during his later years, when his skills as a lawyer began to sharpen, when he had these thoughts of cheating the Devil.

Imagine outwitting Lucifer himself. How did the Bible put it? *For whoever shall call upon the Lord shall be saved.* (Romans 10:13.)

"I also know the Scriptures," the Devil interjected into Luigi's thought process. "That cheap trick has been used in the past, but by those much smarter than you!" Satan was talking through his teeth. He was practically on top of Luigi. Luigi, for the first time, saw an expression he feared—a grin that practically deformed the Devil's face. He could feel the evil radiance of the malignant one.

Luigi felt his left leg go numb and then he felt the prickling of a thousand needles. The tingling sensation turned into a feverous itch.

Luigi discreetly pulled on his left trouser.

Luigi attended to his left calf. Thick, coarse hairs were beginning to protrude from his skin. He could see the hair slowly growing like grass in a stop-action video. This was the beginning of the metamorphosis that would ultimately turn him into a half-goat demon.

Luigi found that he could disrupt the growth of those whiskers by digging into his skin with his nails. Ordinarily this would have been unpleasant but the metamorphosis had desensitized him to pain. The patch of skin with the goat hair would flake off with the proper fingernail to skin action. The cleared space was free of hair for a few seconds before the growing started again.

"As in all fair contracts, ours has an escape clause," said Satan with an evil laugh. "As long as the hair does not make a complete circle around the leg, you will retain your identity. Once the circle is complete, however, you will not be able to prevent the change. The hairs will grow up to your thighs and down to your ankles. Your toes will fuse together and your toenails will grow and expand into a perfect goat hoof, and then you will be my servant."

Satan's face showed no expression. His mouth was frozen in a smile. Laughter was coming out of his eyes. The laughter was loud and diabolic, yet no one seemed to hear. The courtroom business went on without interruption.

The attorney in Luigi began to take control. He had come too far to give in without a fight. If there's an angle, Lou Salby will find a measurement.

His initial anxieties evaporated. He could beat the Devil at this goat hair game. In a few short moments Luigi had developed a rhythm to keep the hairs off his calf by using both hands. With this brief victory he felt a new wave of confidence.

Lou heard himself laugh. It was his trademark chuckle—the laugh that had been the prelude to the doom of countless opponents in the courtroom. He could sense that this ordeal would not last long and he would win.

Then the right leg began to tingle. Luigi felt the same sensation of a thousand needles now pricking his right leg exactly as had occurred to his left leg. Immediately he began to feel the familiar itching. First he fought fear, then he fought the panic that wanted to overpower him.

No, he would not give up. He would use both hands, much faster, more systematically. Luigi heard laughter. He knew the source.

"Are you OK, Mr. Salby?" inquired an associate.

"Oh my God," yelled the stenographer. She was on her feet holding her machine. "Look! His legs are bleeding!" All eyes were on Luigi.

"What's the matter, Lou? Lou? Lou!" The associate was confused as to what to do.

Luigi was scratching like a madman, his fingers bloodied. At the other end of the courtroom the sheriffs were trying to maintain order. The judge pressed his panic button and retired to his chambers. Additional security personnel were on their way.

Luigi ripped his arm away from the associate. What an imbecile, thought Luigi. Can't he see I'm trying to prevent the completion of the circle? All that was needed was a little time. The circle was being neutralized. There was a slight slowdown in the metamorphic process. He could sense it.

"Let go of my arms, you idiots! I have this under control. I can handle it. Leave me alone! Let me go!"

No one understood Luigi's words. He was speaking in a language that only demonologists understood.

Why won't they listen? thought Luigi. He had to prevent the circle. He had to struggle with his associates, who were trying to prevent his hands from reaching his legs. Luigi's strength was giving out. He could use his legs—yes, he would use his legs, and he would not give up.

Luigi kicked savagely. For a moment, he was free. He had to scratch; the circle was almost connecting. He could feel the weight of the security officers immobilizing his arms. At that point, Luigi began to cry.

All those present could hear his sobs. Only Luigi Salvatore heard the laughter. The triumphant laughter that was coming out of Satan's eyes.

7 The Battle at Tita's House
(or How the Devil Defeated Pride and Envy)

The woman howled like an animal from inside her house. It was Tita. She was going through her crazy attacks again. A second howl quickly followed. This time the howl was louder and longer. The sound was more like that made by a wolf than one made by a human.

Tita's husband looked nervously out the window. He was checking to see if anyone had noticed. His wife had gone into these crazy fits in the past; nobody paid much attention to her behavior anymore. Everyone knew that Tita would calm down as quickly as she had flared up.

The husband looked down the dirt road and spied the reverend and his entourage approaching. The reverend was a huge man, the only one wearing a white shirt and tie. His shirt was soaked in sweat, and he was obviously uncomfortable in the heat of the noon sun. The reverend still insisted on the white shirt and dark tie, which he took as the official uniform of the church. This sacrifice had to be made; he had an image to uphold. He was a man of God! He preferred to endure the terrestrial heat than the eternal flames of Hades.

The husband withdrew from the window. He felt embarrassed. He prayed that Tita would be quiet.

It was hot for everyone, not just for the reverend. It was Lent, the height of the dry season. Around the reverend you could see the curious and well-wishers, and surrounding them you could see the radiation of dry heat. The country path was not paved. Where the clay on the road was exposed, it was compacted by the stomping of livestock and the traffic of people. The inevitable orange dust cloud that followed remained constant. The dust had the uncanny effect of magnifying the heat.

For over a month the talk among the adults had been the expected arrival of the reverend. The facts were that this reverend had made a fantastic escape from the island of Cuba. The political leaders of Cuba had just turned his government communist. Now the government was persecuting and exterminating all God-fearing people. The government was specifically targeting the religious leaders of all faiths. The reverend had been identified and caught, with all sorts of unpleasant things happening to him in the hands of the Cuban Gestapo.

Then the reverend had escaped. It was rumored that the walls surrounding his jail cell had actually collapsed, and that his military jailers had fled in terror when he was rescued by angels. The reverend had gone to preaching in the countryside. Even though the reverend kept preaching, all efforts by the government to recapture him were in vain. The reverend would preach the gospel at one location, then disappear, only to miraculously re-appear to preach again at a different locale. The reverend's ultimate arrival to this sister island was being praised as a miracle.

The reverend's wife had preceded the arrival of her husband. She had quickly become the center of discussions about the Cuban communist regime and their barbaric treatment of the faithful. She was instrumental in raising her husband's stature and fueling his fame. She related marvelous accounts of the reverend's imprisonment and torture, of his daring escape past Cuban officials and secret police, and his ultimate miraculous maritime escape past the Cuban gunships.

Regarding Tita, the only one who had dealt with her condition was Madama La Curandera, the healer. Madama's credentials for dealing with Tita were that of being the midwife who had brought Tita into this world. Madama would know more about dealing with Tita's condition than anyone else in existence.

Madama had examined Tita and diagnosed her as being subject to insanity demon attacks. She had prescribed certain baths in a variety of herbs depending on the stages of the moon. She would have Tita drink teas from leaves and roots that were gathered from the local flora and visit periodically to give her neck and head massages with snake and cow udder ointments.

The time came when these treatments did not completely satisfy Tita's family. The family had decided to give modern medicine a chance and took Tita to the village for professional opinions. The town doctors had immediately diagnosed her illness as schizophrenia. Tita was then taken to the capital for further treatment in a specialized medical center. At this clinic, Tita was administered electrical shock treatments and given a variety of pills and medicine.

After all the expended effort, Tita's condition became worse. All the modern scientific advancements had failed to yield results. The attacks not only returned, they were more frequent and of a higher intensity.

Then Tita did something she had never done before. During one of her attacks, she ripped a leg off a live chicken with her teeth. The chicken escaped, leaving Tita in a bloody mess. The family was left in total shock, fully persuaded that taking Tita to the capital had been a mistake. A "giant mistake," just as Madama had predicted.

The family once again turned to Madama the Healer for guidance. The family now was totally convinced that those shock treatments and therapy at the capital had done more harm than good. Madama, on her part, increased the massage treatments and insisted on more expensive herbal ingredients for Tita's ritual baths. Tita now needed more attention as she was entering a stage of violence and lusting for blood.

Tita was in her bedroom sitting on her unmade bed. She had wrapped herself in the white bed sheet, leaving only her face and legs exposed. Her head was tilted upwards; she stared blankly at the ceiling. Her husband reached for her and embraced her, stroking her in a tranquilizing fashion. He made a silent prayer: God, please don't let her scream. Not now, not with the reverend approaching.

Tita could feel the reverend approaching. Somehow the husband knew this. He could sense that Tita would scream. She was building air in her lungs; she would scream her loudest! He tried to force her to lie down. She struggled mildly. He wrestled and covered her mouth with his right hand. He felt her relax, then felt her teeth sink into the palm of his hand. As soon as he eased his grip, Tita ran out of the bedroom making short bursts of horrifying screams until she reached the window. At the window she bellowed a most terrifying howl.

The reverend had already passed the window but was not far from the house. He stopped and turned to face the caller. He knew the call was demonic. He knew the challenge was for him. A battle was to begin.

Madama the Healer contemplated the arrival of the long-awaited reverend from across a shallow gully. She stood tall in the entrance of her home, arms crossed in anger, angry at a man she had never met. How this anger had turned to hate she did not know. When or how the seeds of envy were planted, she could not remember. Maybe what she initially felt was a form of professional jealousy. She had always been the undisputed physical and spiritual healer of the area. Her knowledge in botany and horology was extensive. She commanded a high degree of respect in this field of medicine, her services being the only bastion of first aid available to those falling sick in her domain.

In the realm of the occult, Madama had a secured place. The religious and the non- believers alike either applauded her or were careful with her. They all had an opinion, and all would err on the side of caution. It was common knowledge that Madama was blessed with the "gift." She had proven on more than one occasion that a supernatural force was within her.

Prior to the arrival of this reverend, Madama had never felt the desire for fame or attention. Yet she wanted the notoriety and attention that the reverend was getting. She had never jealously guarded her stature. Today she would be on guard so that her worth would not diminish. She knew that the envy she felt was not of God. Maybe this lust would go away; she wanted it to go away. She knew, however, that her feelings would remain the same as long as the reverend stayed in her domain.

The reverend was absorbing all the attention like a peacock. All the commotion was not his doing, that was true, but the reverend was not doing anything to constrain the masses. A true man of God would show some control, Madama thought. At that moment, Madama concluded that this man was a fraud, a charlatan who had to be exposed for the sake of her Christian children. The reverend's arrival had been too pompous; it was a defiance to her rightful position. He was a disciple of the malignant one, sent precisely to disrupt the spiritual harmony of the naïve. This reverend was the biblical wolf in sheep's clothing.

Do not let your heart envy sinners. That's what the book of Proverbs says. Madama knew she was wrong. She was sinning. She could feel a corroding in her soul.

Madama had heard the screams as she observed the reverend and his following parade. Now she was watching the whole procession stop at Tita's house. She could see the reverend in the front line; he was addressing the household, then the masses. Whatever he was up to, it was no good. He could do what he wanted, but not at Tita's house.

Madama, with a newfound purpose, reached for her cane and, with effort, forced her arthritic knees down her hill, which would put her on the path to Tita's house.

The reverend walked to the front of the small zinc-walled house. The house was simple, built above the ground on stilts. In the savage heat, the house appeared to sway. The reverend noticed that the leaves of the trees and palms were still. There was no breeze, no bird or insect making noise. This was the Devil's work. He must not weaken.

The doors, like all the windows of the house, were wide open. The reverend could see the house radiate heat against the blue sky. With the authority of a man of God, the reverend climbed the steps to the entrance. The reverend could feel the oven-like heat escape from the house.

The reverend walked into the house without being invited. He stood tall at the entrance of the home. This giant man looked past the small figure of Tita's husband and fixed his sights on Tita. His eyes squinted. He could feel the heat emitted by the house and the woman.

How rude, thought the small man, who was now made to feel inconsequential in his own home. Where were the customary greetings, the Christian salutations? He was still the man of his own house. He flushed with embarrassment. His house, his health, and his Tita all belonged to God, and wasn't this God's servant? Was this interloper the answer to his prayers?

The reverend had eyes only for Tita. He had no time to deal with the insignificant man. He viewed his challenge as coming from Satan—a challenge that he would meet anywhere. He didn't feel the need to ask permission to enter the house. A higher calling had endowed him with the authority to dispense with his courtesies to others. This house was possessed. He had a mandate from God; his knee would bow to no man. He felt superior.

Tita's husband, nervous, embarrassed, anxious, and overcome by the authority of this interloper, gave way and, standing aside, allowed this reincarnated Moses to enter his house.

The reverend called loudly to his wife for his Bible and for his bottle of anointing oil. He was leaving no doubts about his intentions; he was going to pray at the site. There would be a battle in this house!

The reverend stared at Tita. He would not be intimidated by a malignant force. Tita grinned back, hissing from behind her teeth, her head and body dancing with the motions of a charmed cobra. The trance was broken by the commotion caused by the approaching Madama the Healer. Her steps were forceful and deliberate. She addressed the gathering loudly as she approached the house.

"The day of judgment on this house has come!" Madama walked closer to the house. "Stand back and stay clear! The screams you now hear are not of this world. Tita has been possessed by a malevolent force. You must all get back. A released demon can easily possess the next closest human. Confirm this, reverend!" yelled Madama as she pointed her cane at the reverend, who was once again by the door.

Madama had the advantage. The reverend did not have prior knowledge of who Madama was. He hesitated. The mysterious woman was right. This was the work of demons, and they will roam until they find another soul to possess.

"It's true, a demon will possess you, but only if you are not fortified by our Lord Jesus Christ," the reverend responded from the door entrance. His voice was again commanding authority.

Who was this woman? Who had sent her to interfere with his calling? He knew he must act quickly; his flock would not stay together for long with this intrusion. He could sense the demon of confusion beginning to take effect on his people. He calculated this woman to be another demon-possessed witch from this demon-infested area. This was why the Lord had directed his steps to this unholy island, to free these Christian souls from Satan's grip.

Madama had been successful in imparting a sense of danger and urgency. The masses began to disband. The children and young people were already at a distance. The older folk were cautiously still moving.

Madama had succeeded in breaking the hold the reverend had on her children. Those remaining consisted only of the reverend's wife and two brothers in the faith who felt firm in their holy ways.

Madama rested on her cane. She contemplated the results with satisfaction. The reverend continued to support himself on the door frame. The sun reflected from the beads of sweat that had formed on his face. The heat coming from inside the house was unbearable. The reverend looked visibly annoyed. He had not counted on Madama. He stared at her; he would have to deal with this abomination. This he would do in God's name.

Madama, staring at the reverend, had similar thoughts. In God's name she would have to deal with this imposter. She thought about challenging the reverend by asking on whose authority he cast out demons, on whose authority he could waltz into strangers' homes and lives? On whose authority?

Too late! The reverend, properly focused as a man with a mission, took advantage of Madama's hesitation. He called out to his wife. He called out to the two loyal brothers and made his way directly toward Tita.

The Devil himself started making the noises and screams that followed out of Tita's mouth. She wiggled like a serpent. She spat, screamed, and kicked with an apparent endless source of energy. She was a small woman with the strength of a robust man. The brothers and the reverend's wife were busy trying to restrain Tita. Even with the makeshift restraining jacket made from the bed sheet that Tita had wrapped around herself, it was difficult to keep her down. Tita wrestled free, only to be captured again by the reverend and his faithful. The three men and the reverend's wife were beginning to show fatigue. The heat was exhausting them.

Tita's husband had observed enough. He made his way toward the group and joined in holding Tita down. His voice also joined in the choir of prayers being elevated for Tita's deliverance.

Madama was now left alone, but she would not be outdone. She abruptly left, heading down the path toward the "Y" at the bottom of the hill that would take her back to her house. She went back to her house, but not in retreat. She went home to prepare for battle. She also was a woman with a mission.

Minutes later, she was heading back up the hill toward the battle at Tita's house. Madama's steps were slower this time and she was relying a lot more on her cane. She had changed into a simple white cotton dress with a light blue satchel wrapped around her waist. Hanging from her shoulder was an open pouch carrying large herbal bunches of sábila, poleo, and albahaca. She was puffing away on a cigar. With one hand she supported herself on her cane and with the other hand she held a ceremonial maraca.

The single maraca was a work of art. It was larger than an ordinary maraca. This maraca was the size of a bowling ball. It had faces carved on it as well as other symbols and figures. The handle was an ordinary cut-off broomstick that had been elaborately doctored for religious ceremonial purposes. The maraca was further adorned by seven rosaries intertwined at the top, made of rosary beads of different sizes and colors, giving it an impressive appearance.

Madama knew she had in her hand a formidable weapon against

any type of evil spirit. The maraca had been her ally—an ally that had never failed her. She held her maraca high as she approached the house. The silver crucifixes were glittering in the sun. Without breaking stride, and chanting words in an alien dialect, she rattled the maraca at the house on stilts, walked up the few steps, and entered the battle.

She paid no attention to the efforts of the reverend and his cronies. Up to now, their efforts had been in vain. She stepped around them, tall, erect, proud, and puffing away at what was once a giant cigar. The thick, strong aroma of the cigar filled the room. The smoke added heat to the existing oven.

It was easy for Madama to circle the group. They had gravitated toward the center of the room while struggling with Tita. The few humble pieces of furniture had been placed or kicked toward the walls of the small living room. In a corner, she discovered a puddle and broken glass. Someone's vase of holy water had been smashed. The reverend's efforts were going backwards. God was on her side. She would succeed in rescuing Tita from the grip of Satan and the grip of the reverend.

Madama continued walking in circles around the reverend and Tita. The voices of the reverend's group began to lower, the heat beginning to take its toll. As Madama circled and puffed, she also began to swat the walls with the herbal arrangements she had produced from her pouch.

The reverend had it all wrong, Madama thought, as she added a chant to her swatting with the albahaca and sábila. The reverend was trying to extract the demons from Tita directly. That was a plain error. Madama knew that the demons were intertwined with the household. The house itself had to be softened in order for the exorcism to succeed. The added cigar smoke was supposed to chase away the bad spirits. The reverend was just shouting prayers that would not be heard. He was doing nothing. This would be her day.

For a moment, her thoughts were distracted. In her soul she felt she was not right with her God. She quickly made a self-analysis as to the purity of her thoughts. Why am I giving so much of my attention to the reverend? Why so much hatred? she thought. This was unlike her.

It was the seed of envy that was bearing fruit, corroding and possessing her being. She felt unclean. She shouldn't be dealing with unclean spirits if she herself was not in good standing. She tried to set these thoughts aside. She pressed forward. These thoughts were Satan's deliberate efforts to weaken her faith. The Lord had chosen her to deliver the day and put the reverend to shame.

During one of the brief rest spells, one of the brethren lowered his guard and released his hold on one of Tita's arms. The reverend was deep in thought and prayer. He did not see the blow coming.

The punch caught the reverend on the bridge of his nose, raised him to his feet, and hurled him backwards across the room. The reverend's arms were frantically reaching out, making wild gestures, as he tried to get his balance. The reverend grabbed nothing but air as he hit the wall hard with the back of his head. Slowly he slid to the floor, holding his face with one hand and the back of his head with the other.

The reverend thought he would pass out. It was difficult for him to focus. The heat was suffocating. He gasped for air. He could hear the frenzy of prayers. He didn't want attention. The attention should stay centered on the job of liberating Tita from her demons.

The reverend took the momentary hiatus to gather his composure. He hoped that no one would notice his confusion. He was curled in a corner. The bump on the back of his head was beginning to swell. His nose kept bleeding uncontrollably. First his face, then his head, then his whole body protested in pain. He could move, but only with extensive effort. Any movement meant great pain. Where was his anointing oil? How was he to continue the battle against the satanic forces?

The heat in the house felt heavy. The reverend's wife took command; she raised her voice higher than the others in prayer. Through his blurry eyes, the reverend saw the vial of anointing oil in her hand. He thought he felt a cool breeze cut through the dry, asphyxiating heat. The reverend was mistaken; what he was feeling was a flush that was spearing through his body, a wave of nausea, a wave of lightheadedness, a wave that lifted him and gently set him down where he would ultimately lose consciousness. God, he didn't want to faint!

He had to fight the Devil.

Again he made an effort to move. He just wanted to move the blood-soaked handkerchief in his hand away from his face. His effort was useless. The pain was unbearable. He contemplated for the first time his bloodstained shirt. It was saturated in perspiration. The heat was tremendous, as was the pitch of the prayer meeting in the house. His wife was bravely praying, her hands on the demon-possessed Tita, confronting the diabolical forces. Madama was also loudly chanting and going through her exorcism ritual. Two female gladiators, in different directions, with one common goal: demanding Tita's release from the demonic powers.

The reverend tried to move again. Using the wall as a brace, he willed his legs to raise him from his humiliation. His elbows and knees wobbled. He felt nauseated. He felt unbalanced. He did not want to suffer the embarrassment of falling. Slowly, he eased himself back to the floor. His vision was now gone and so was his energy and his desire to continue his fight against the Prince of Evil. What he wanted to do now was to rest.

The pause would only be for a moment. His duty was to free the slave from the bondage of Satan. That was his calling, his mission. He could not back down. He had to demonstrate for all present his true God. He could not go down in disgrace. It was his place to shame Madama, to dishonor that false prophet Madama and the Gods that she worshipped. His God was more powerful than Madama's God! What he wanted was a cool breeze and to stay still, in silence. Thinking of these things, the reverend did not notice his soiled pants before he drifted into unconsciousness.

Madama saw the reverend slam against the wall, saw blood on the reverend's face and fingers. She saw the reverend in defeat, his face on the floor, in the dust. Her heart felt jubilant. She chanted with a newfound fervor, deliberately raising her pitch until it was above all the voices in the room. She swatted the herbal branches in all directions, her ceremonial maraca held high in triumph and thanksgiving.

Those outside heard a wail, as if in death. The heat inside was incredible. The zinc house seemed to be swaying, as if its roof wanted to float off its foundation; some would later testify that the house actually moved in terror.

Inside the house, Madama's jubilation was short-lived. When she raised her maraca in triumph, the malignant spirits were drained from Tita and drawn into Madama's body and soul through the maraca. It was as if she had struck an angry Satan who had come to investigate the disturbance in one of his chosen.

The maraca now had a life of its own. It did not need Madama to rattle it. High above her head, the maraca gave Madama two quick jerks. Madame's chanting turned to screams of terror. She tried to open her fingers to release the maraca. The maraca held fast. Her wrist felt as if it would break.

Madama felt her hair on fire. In a frenzy, she began to put out the flames with her free hand. Again the maraca jerked her, envious that all of Madama's attention was not focused on it. The rosaries were causing their own vibrations. The maraca was rattling Madama. A crucifix snapped off from a rosary and its accompanying beads started to fly off the maraca. The vibrations were electrifying. The maraca was now the master, Madama the tool.

The legion of demons now possessed this holy maraca. The maraca, in turn, possessed Madama. The malignant forces acting through the maraca gave Madama another torturing jerk. Then Madama was jerked again, her elbow snapping with an infernal sound. Madama the Healer screamed in pain and horror, but she could not let go.

With another snap by the maraca, Madama landed on top of Tita and the reverend's wife. All of the humans were immobilized. Only the demonic spirits were at work, tormenting the possessed Madama. The maraca remained erect, reaching toward the ceiling. It appeared as if it were trying to escape but for the clutches of Madama's wasted grasp.

All attentions were on the maraca, which kept a vertical position in Madama's hand. The maraca seemed to glow; it rattled noises not of this world. Madama was becoming a limp carcass, her energies drained by the maraca.

Those watching saw Madama fly out of the house. They claim

that Madama's feet never touched the front steps of the house. She jumped out like an Olympic broad jumper, her legs moving as if trying to find traction in midair. Her arm was stretched out, holding the rattling maraca perfectly straight, as if holding a torch. Her other hand was frantically swatting away the tormenting wasps from hell that only she could see and feel in her hair.

She was running when she landed. She lost a sandal on impact, but did not break stride. She kept running down the hill, the same way she had arrived, down the hill toward the "Y" on the road that would lead her to her house.

For days after the exorcism, the area was not quite the same. Madama never made it back to her house. Scores of her faithful and concerned neighbors took up the search, but Madama was not found. She was never found or heard from again. Her house stayed opened and unattended. No one dared go in or near the house, even after police conducted their investigations. The police did come, and the detectives did investigate, but she was not heard of again. Madama's house ultimately tilted and collapsed in disrepair.

The only things ever recovered were Madama's sandals. One sandal was found close to Tita's house. The other sandal was found at the bottom of the hill where the road bends and makes the "Y" in two directions. Madama was observed going down the hill, but no one saw her come up either of the two roads.

As for Tita, she was taken into custody and admitted to a psychiatric institution by the authorities. At first, she had been arrested because "someone had to be arrested." She was charged with being a prime mover in the disappearance of Madama, but the charges were later dropped. All the witnesses at the inquest testified that Tita had never left her house. A few days later, the psychiatric institutions released Tita after pronouncing her completely healed but uncontrollable.

The consensus of all those timid souls who witnessed the battle at Tita's house was that it was through the prayers and efforts of the reverend's wife that Tita was ultimately healed. The humbleness of his wife had held firm.

For the events of that day the reverend would get no credit. No explanation would be accepted for the cowardly posture that the reverend had taken after being hit in the face. The prevailing consensus was that the reverend was a fraud, that he had never actually seen the Devil, that he had never really been in the presence of true malignant forces. In the face of evil he had cowardly backed away, and at the sight of the Devil he had wet and soiled his pants.

In fairness to the reverend, his nose had been broken in four places by the blow to his face. That was the reason the bleeding would not stop. It would take months before he would fully recover from the injury and much longer to recover from his disgraceful defeat.

In any event, this pompous reverend had lost face. He left in shame, wrapped in the cloth of humility—humility that he recognized he had failed to show. He left thanking his most merciful God that he had been given a second chance, the chance that had been denied to Madama la Curandera.

8 The Five Gold Krugerrands

Kenny's father passed away without incident. The funeral arrangement was simple and few people came. It took Kenny's sister almost six weeks to find Kenny and tell him the news about their father's passing. Then Kenny was only found because of the intervention and involvement of the local chapter of the Salvation Army. It had not been the first time this religious army had come in contact with Kenny and his family.

Kenny and the Salvation Army members had the usual relationship. To the army, Kenny was a man in need of much prayer, a man who required a lot of patience to deal with. Kenny, on the other hand, tolerated the affectionate attention offered by the church members. Tolerated because it was attention he did not seek. He tolerated it as an ingredient freely given whenever he accepted a handout or a bowl of warm soup.

Kenny's sister had neatly divided his dad's earthly possession. Brothers-in-law had gotten a few tools. Sister had kept the balance of the $7,500 life insurance policy after the funeral expenses. All that was left in dad's estate was given to Kenny in a cloth pouch: six gold South

African Krugerrands.

Gold was at approximately $400 an ounce, so the coins were worth about $2,400. Kenny would later find out the actual value of the Krugerrands when he came across a discarded copy of the Wall Street Journal. For the moment, Kenny felt content with his sister's handling of his dad's affairs. As always, sister found a way to equitably divide what was to be distributed. He just did not appreciate the way his inheritance was handed to him. The pouch had actually been tossed to him. Six gold coins, how clever and appropriate.

His sister was right. He had never given any thought to the possibility of his father not being around. Initially, he was numbed by the news of his dad's death. Then he cried, and kept on crying. The crying was uncontrollable; the tears kept on rolling. He tried to make sense of it all but the rational kept escaping him.

Kenny felt a loss, not the loss of not having his father with him anymore. That was his fault. He had chosen this nomadic life of the streets. The decision to divorce himself from the affection of his dad and family had been made ages ago. Kenny had left his home, never measuring the worth of the warmth and affection that his family circle offered against the cold street and his passion for the bottle. More than once he had contemplated the irrationality of his election processes, but always he had been able to rationalize his choice. How could God punish a sick mortal, a man without control? How could his dad blame him for having been born with so little will power against the sweet taste of cheap fruit wine?

The loss he felt was for the lack of direction he had with his life. This realization had been accented by the recent news of his father's death. On that account, he felt real sadness. Kenny remembered well that it was his father who had first pointed this fact out to him: "You must control your actions; you are special in God's eyes! The Lord has given you life for a purpose! Your life has a meaning. You will do meaningful things, but you must have focus. You must have direction."

How do you argue the topic of God's existence with your father? Or the purpose of man's existence? How could he explain that man's existence precedes his essence? Kenny had once told his dad to read Sartre. Man had not been created by God for a purpose or by anyone else for any purpose. Man just existed!

Kenny had made a conscious effort to stay clear of the preaching of his father. Still, he seemed to always gravitate toward those "brothers in the faith" of the Salvation Army. How could he convince others that God did not exist if he wasn't clear on the concept himself?

Years later, while Kenny was still diving into the abyss of alcoholism, a young officer in the Salvation Army had pointed this very condition out to him, that he was living a life without direction, a life without meaning. How he hated their preaching! But the preaching came with the scarf, the cup of hot coffee, and a refuge when the winter nights were coldest.

Now he finds himself armed with six gold coins, and somehow he's supposed to make sense out of his life as if the coins possessed some cosmic meaning. Is the inheritance of these gold coins a milestone in my life? he thought. The fact that he was even thinking about the coins, his life, his father, bothered him. It was as if his father were making his presence felt through the coins. As if a message were being sent to him from the afterlife. A message that Kenny had a mandate, that he was put forth on this earth for a purpose. That a "meaningful act" was expected from him and must be done.

Kenny felt a great weight on his conscience. His inner being craved the habitual remedy of all his ailments. Yes, that's what he needed, a good stiff drink. With the pleasantry of this thought, Kenny made a direct line to the local coin shop where he would explore the chance to redeem the gold coins for legal tender.

The effects of the whisky did not completely drown out Kenny's sentiments. Something had to be done to that common criminal masquerading as a coin dealer. Kenny felt angry at himself for allowing the coin shop merchant to take advantage of him. The merchant must have read in his eyes that the proceeds would be used for the purchase of liquor. Kenny had been offered, and he had accepted, $150 for a coin that was easily worth double that amount. To make matter worse, the dealer had acted as if he was doing Kenny a favor. As if Kenny was acting out of desperation for a fix of heroin or cocaine. As if Kenny had no rightful claim to the coin, as if the coin was stolen!

Kenny had tried to explain that the coin was holy, a bequeath from his dad, a dying gift to be respected. Nothing had moved that Shylock. Kenny had been treated like a *bum*. A flush of anger and frustration overcame him. The grown man cried again.

This day would come. The Salvation Army preacher had predicted it. Could this be the lowest level that he could reduce himself to? Could his sins drag him down any lower?

"You have to make him pay for his blatant act of disrespect." Yes, that was what his father was telling him to do! He was hearing his dad clearly.

Not to worry, he will pay. That cheat would not remain unpunished. In time, Kenny would get him. Now was not the appropriate moment to even the score, though. That's how the mind is made to error. That's how he had recently ended up in jail, by rushing and not thinking his actions out. Kenny would get even, but he would not rush it. With enough time he would think of a punishment for that boy, something imaginative, something that would make his papa proud.

"Don't rush me!" he yelled at his dad. "I told you I'll get him." A bystander quickened his pace. All he could see was a demented vagabond talking gibberish to himself and swinging at his shadow. To Kenny, however, the shadow was real.

If only his father would stop looking at him, he could gather his thoughts. Kenny attacked the imaginary figure of his father. On impact, two other heads appeared from behind the head of his father. His dad had transformed into the three-headed monster, Cerberus. Cerberus had left his place of sentry in hell and had come for Kenny, to drag Kenny to the circle of hell where the sin of drunkenness is punished.

A mood of self-pity came over Kenny. He would plead for mercy. He had no faults, no evil heart. It was by impulse, not by malice, that he sinned. Would his maker be anguished by his torment, like the

78

pity Dante had for the Florentine named Ciacco?

Kenny's mood then changed to anger. He tried to scratch his father's eyes out. He did not succeed. The exercise did not make him feel better, only fatigued. The frigid air of the evening finally brought him back to his senses. At a distance he could make out a Salvation Army bell ringer making a boring motion with her bell.

Kenny contemplated the empty bottle of whisky and properly discarded it in a trash bin. He had been drinking brand names since he came into his mini-fortune. He had one small bottle left and he cradled this treasure close to his heart.

Then Kenny saw them: Popeye and Billy Ray! There was no time for evasive action. Kenny, in his daydream, had practically stumbled on these two demons.

Like vultures on the scent of a fresh cadaver, Popeye and Billy Ray appeared to stalk him. These two wine heads were fearless psychos. They had robbed Kenny in the past. At one time or another, almost everyone in their subculture had been victimized by this duo. The last time they assaulted Kenny they had almost broken his neck. The gash on his head had taken twenty stitches to close and the police had done nothing.

Kenny was gripped by terror. How could these demons possibly know he had coins of value, money, and whiskey?

Popeye's name was not a misnomer. He had been hit in the face with a concrete block. His face had been smashed inwards, flattening his left eyeball while forcing his right eyeball outwards from its socket. Popeye's grotesque disfigurement was only overshadowed by the unpleasantness of his demeanor.

Billy Ray was either just plain mean or completely burnt out by the vice of alcohol. In any case, Billy Ray had reached a stage of not being able to function like a human being. He lived merely for the pleasures of drinking. Being in an inebriated state was the only thing that kept him sedately civilized. He had been stabbed many times. Being a big fellow, he actually welcomed the chance to inflict pain or have pain inflicted on him. Drunk or not, Billy Ray was not interested in peace.

There was no doubt in Kenny's mind that Popeye and Billy Ray were coming to get him. He had been singled out. Maybe it was the vivacious scent of new liquor on his breath.

Popeye was almost upon him; Kenny's heart was pounding furiously. All is lost, he thought, my money, my inheritance, my chance at doing a meaningful act. Kenny knew how meticulous these two could be when searching for their victims. It now seemed obvious that selling one of the coins had been a mistake and this was his punishment. He may have caused damage that could not be repaired. By separating the coins, he had upset their harmony. The collective powers of the coins had been reduced by one sixth. This is foolish, Kenny thought, I'm personalizing these gold coins.

Popeye was now on him, piercing Kenny with his demonic eye. "Are you holding out on us, Kenny boy?"

Billy Ray grasped Kenny's arm from behind while Popeye snatched a brown paper bag from Kenny's hand. Popeye opened the bag and pulled out his reward—a fifth of V.O. As if by paternal instinct, Kenny reached back for his baby. His effort and protest were quickly swatted away. Kenny fell hard on the concrete sidewalk.

The duo's focus was now on their newfound prize. They were obsessed with the brand new bottle. Their thoughts of checking Kenny's pockets were no longer paramount. The attention was on starting their feast. Kenny, finally realizing his good fortune, made haste in the opposite direction.

Kenny found himself rushing away. His escape from Popeye and Billy Ray was nothing less than an act of God. Kenny was now among the curious, those who had witnessed the incident but had not interfered. On the contrary, it was amusing to watch three drunks fighting over a bottle of V.O from a distance.

Kenny had been contemplating what would be his "'meaningful act." He had been vacillating; now he came to the realization that he had another chance. The power of the coins was still intact.

An extraordinary act he would do, and the key was the coins.

Why else would his dad leave these coins to cross his path? He would stun the world, make them all take notice. His father would be proud. The captain of the Salvation Army would approve. During his sober moments he analyzed his position like the Harvard graduate in business administration that he was.

Kenny touched the cloth pouch hidden inside his shirt. He felt the coins. They were no longer cold next to his body. They were not only warm, they felt alive. He could feel the pulse of each individual coin as easily as he could feel the ridges of their uncirculated edges. It was during this moment when he felt the life force of the conjoined coins. It was at this moment that he had a vision of how he would act.

The plan was simple. The coins would be secretly deposited in a Salvation Army Christmas contribution pail. This would undoubtedly start a fad, which could easily graduate into a season tradition. The Salvation Army could sensationalize the incident by concentrating on solving the mystery of the gold coin contributor. The public would be looking for a collector of coins or a wealthy person. Newspapers would expand the search. Real philanthropists would copy and start anonymously dropping gold coins in the holiday buckets.

Kenny smiled at his cleverness. So many people owning gold coins, and this had not been done before, even though baby Jesus was presented with gold on the very first Christmas.

This had the making of a tradition the Salvation Army would want to continue. After a while, the phenomenon would be expected. Bell ringers throughout the city would make prayers for their pails to be blessed and for their efforts to be rewarded by finding a valuable coin. Legends would be created! The possibilities seemed endless. One thing was certain—secrecy was of the essence.

Kenny checked his pockets. He was down to his last four dollars. There was no hesitation. He carefully wrapped three gold Krugerrands with three dollar bills. He contemplated the irony of it all. On the one hand, he had hundreds of dollars, and then on the other hand, he didn't even have enough dollar bills to wrap each gold coin separately. He proceeded to wrap the last two coins with the last dollar bill of his inheritance. He walked directly to the corner bell ringer and dropped the wrapped coins in the red bucket.

The young raw recruit, properly bundled in her regulation uniform coat, did not notice Kenny's charitable act. Her "thank you" and "God bless you" were for anyone who came close enough to hear her. She continued her monotonous bell ringing as she wished him a Merry Christmas. She felt safe. This smelly fellow in rags could not get far if he tried to steal her contribution pail. The area was crowded with holiday shoppers. Besides, she was certain she had the protection of God's angels.

Kenny started to make his way toward the Salvation Army shelter. The young Salvation Army cadet's face came to mind and he wondered how that particular bell ringer had gotten started in the religion cause.

Kenny quickened his pace. He had two or three other ideas that he could implement with the help of the brothers in the Salvation Army. With God's help, I could stay sober and think up a couple more visions, Kenny thought.

Kenny was crying again. The tears and the cold wind on his face did not matter. There was joy in his heart. Kenny found himself running toward the sanctuary of the Salvation Army shelter, running with a newfound determination to do what was right. He was running toward the hope of a new life. At last, some focus and direction!

The young lady, still wearing her Salvation Army cadet uniform, stood paralyzed over the kitchen table. Her mother had emptied the contents of the contribution pail on the table to count the day's proceeds. They never imagined they would be counting gold coins. The four small children that shared the cramped apartment had gathered around the two adults. The children could sense that something was amiss. They watched the two adults in silence, too young to fully comprehend the soundless excitement.

It was the matriarch who broke the quietude. She quickly made her daughter and grandchildren make a circle around the humble kitchen table. The old lady, with her whole family now holding hands, elevated a prayer of thanksgiving. The prayer started in a low voice and then worked its way to a loud crescendo as the rest of the family joined in the jubilation.

The grandma's delight was not only for the newfound wealth. Not at all. In the beginning of the Christmas season, grandma had felt uncomfortable getting her daughter to masquerade as a Salvation Army bell ringer. She had even felt some fear for the Lord's wrath. It felt like stealing. In her heart, she felt it was wrong, but her circumstances, her family's needs, her unanswered prayers… If only the Lord would send her a sign.

The greater joy the old lady felt was for the sign that the Lord, in his infinite mercy, had bestowed on her. The Lord had sent her the coins as a sign and a blessing, sent only to those God-fearing servants worthy of His grace. Her fears and worries had been unfounded. The idea of impersonating a Salvation Army bell ringer had not been an evil one, as she had previously thought. Thanks to this heavenly benediction, this year they would have a Merry Christmas indeed.

9 Dinner With Grandma

"Grandma, I'm going to take you out for dinner," I happily informed my granny as I passed by her on my way to the bedroom where I usually threw my school books. I didn't receive the response I was expecting; I didn't receive a response at all!

I bounced right into that kitchen, tapped her on the rump, and reiterated, "Hey baby lucks, I'm taking you out to dinner." This time I grabbed her. My face was flush in her face. I could smell the aroma of every possible Latin American spice intertwined in her silver hair. Her cooking had no equal! To this day, I consider her cooking the best on this globe.

"Why?" she answered softly as she consciously wiped her hands on her food-stained apron. She was now looking at me, somewhat annoyed that I had interrupted the rhythm of her cooking. "I have already fixed dinner."

All the air was let out of my balloon. I was expecting a totally different answer, like the responses I was becoming accustomed to getting when I threw this line at the girls at the university. It wasn't often that I saved enough to go out on a dinner date.

"I didn't mean today, grandma," I lied.

"You know I'm too old for this going out business. Young people really don't want to be seen with us old folks anyways."

I ignored the comment. "I was going to say that maybe we can go out tomorrow," I lied. "Gee, we can go out whenever you get a chance."

"What's the matter, child? You don't like my cooking anymore?" she asked. She had a piercing stare. That grandma stare that captivates, the stare that challenges even the thought of the unthinkable, the thought of crossing that line of disrespect.

"You know I love your cooking. This has nothing to do with your cooking. Don't try twisting me out of the topic like you did last Mother's Day. I just want to take you out for a change! We can drive out to the capital, we can hit a restaurant..."

"Well, I don't know," she said.

"You don't know what? You don't know if you want to go, or you don't know the restaurant you want to go to?" I mocked her.

"Why do you really want to go out to the restaurant?" she said softly. "I can prepare for you anything that you would like right here."

"That's just it! I don't want you to prepare anything. On the contrary, I want someone else to prepare food for you. We can have someone else wait on us for a change."

"I don't mind serving you. The opposite is true. I like being at your service. I wouldn't be doing it if it caused me too great of a discomfort." I noted the tenderness in her voice as she touched my cheek.

"Besides," she said, the sweetness in her voice now gone, "I prefer to see the food before I cook it. Make sure it's washed before it's cooked and definitely see it before I eat it. Trust me, there's a reason the store doesn't want us to see the actual food preparation. Go on and sit, dinner is almost done."

"Think of it; you won't have to cook," I said, ignoring her last comment.

"I always have to cook. The others eat here too, you know. Besides, I don't mind cooking, really I don't."

"Think of it, grandma. You can take the day off. You won't have to cook for anyone. You can do something you like," I shot back.

"Something I like?" she asked in her soft voice again.

"Yes," was my quick response, my arms in the air in victory.

"I like to cook," she said, staring at the ceiling. "I like my kitchen." She was nodding her head, agreeing with herself. "These are the things I like..."

Grandma was being difficult. Now she was walking away, shaking her head side to side.

"Please, sit down for supper!" She was being stern again. I was losing her. "If you stop talking nonsense and sit down, I will be able to finish your dinner."

"Come on, Grandma, this is not that hard. All I want to do is take...you...out...to... *dinner!*" I waved my arms in agitation. I had to change my technique. "All you have to do is simply get in the Beetle Bug and we can calmly drive out to a quiet place to eat."

I was making some headway, I could sense it. I was gaining ground. My granny was smiling now, taking long breaths. I pressed the attack.

"I'm just looking to take my best girl out to eat," I continued. "Nothing sinful about that, is there?" Excellent choice of words. Always throw a little church into the argument. If it's not sinful it has to be good. I think I got her!

"What restaurant did you have in mind, sweetie?" she asked.

"We can go to any restaurant you like," I quickly responded. "We can go whenever and wherever you like." Finally! Victory in sight!

"You don't know who does the cooking in these places, do you?" She asked while serving me.

"No… Come on grandma, we don't even know where we're going yet."

"You probably don't know how the food is prepared either, do you?" I got that change of voice again. "You don't know about the condition of their kitchen, or if they clean the vegetables before preparing them. Or if they let the flies land on the food. Haven't you noticed that the food is not prepared in front of you? Why do you suppose that the kitchens are always in the back, eh? I'm not sure what they want to hide, but I'm sure they want to hide something. That's why they have to go to the back and cook the food."

I couldn't believe my ears. What logic!

"You have no idea whose filthy hands are going to prepare the food you want us to eat. Yes, it's true, you don't know if they wash their hands. Only our Lord knows what they do with their hands when they go to the toilet. You really don't expect me to sit down and enjoy the food made in those roach-infested kitchens, do you?"

"No ma'am, you are very mistaken. These kitchens don't have any roaches. I'm not going to take you to a roach-infested restaurant," I protested. Grandma was not listening; now she was not letting me speak.

"You are a very smart university boy," she said, tapping my head as she finished serving me my supper, "but I know more than you about kitchens. Believe me, they have their roaches as sure as rice is white." Then she pushed my chair closer to the table, inspected the silverware, then placed the fork in my palm. "Eat." That was the end of the dialogue.

As I finished the last mouthful on my plate, I became aware that the smell of rice and beans from the kitchen was being replaced by the overpowering fragrance of Jean Nate.

"Do I look OK for a drive, son?" she asked in a little girlish voice. "I still like ice creams." There she stood, straight as a soldier in front of the table. She was wiping facial powder off her glasses. She had no makeup on, just a lot of powder. It was obvious she had put it on in haste. Her apron had disappeared, replaced by a pastel-blue flower print dress. She was holding her oversized bag in the classical grandma fashion, with both hands gripping the top, as if the bag was full of canaries ready to escape.

Another wave of Jean Nate filled my nostrils. I was in love. She looked marvelous in her simple cotton dress. I couldn't remember the last time I had seen her without that regulation apron on. In my heart I felt an added sense of appreciation for that lady. For a good moment I merely contemplated her, just soaking in the radiance of her presence, and in that moment of silent meditation I thanked God for my good fortune. I wanted to hug her but my arms were busy doing gymnastics around my eyes. I wasn't about to let her see her smart college 'macho' with tears in his eyes.

That evening we did go out. I drove her out to the capital, San Juan. She had two scoops of coconut ice cream. I ate the chocolate cone.

David Delgado

10 State vs. Bloom

This case may sound fantastic, but it actually happened. The facts as presented are in essence the same. The players really existed. Their identities have been disguised in order to protect the innocent. It was reported by the Criminal Bulletin Press that this drama unfolded itself with almost identical facts. Incredible but true.

This is what happened: Mrs. Bloom, seventy-six years of age, was accused of retail theft and assault and battery upon an employee, to wit Mr. Hobbs of Goldbrick's Department Store.

The accounting of what happened takes us directly to the courthouse and into the middle of the trial. All witnesses wait outside of the court room until it is their turn to testify. The major witnesses will be examined and enough information given so that you, the reader, can decide the defendant's guilt or innocence.

These are the charges the people of the State of Illinois (The State) must prove:

Assault: A person commits an assault when, without lawful authority, he engages in conduct which places another in reasonable apprehension of receiving a battery.

Battery: A person commits battery if he intentionally or knowingly without legal justification and by any means, (1) causes bodily harm to an individual or (2) makes physical contact of an insulting or provoking nature with an individual.

Retail Theft: A person commits the offense of retail theft when he knowingly takes possession of, carries away, transfers, or causes to be carried away or transferred, any merchandise displayed, held, stored, or offered for sale in a retail mercantile establishment with the intention of retaining such merchandise or with the intention of depriving the merchant permanently of the possession or use of benefit of such merchandise without paying the full retail value for such merchandise.

The defense team decided that Mrs. Bloom would not make a good witness. She would not be called to testify on her own behalf. Note that, in our judicial system, a defendant (Mrs. Bloom) does not have to take the stand in her defense, as the State has the burden of proving the defendant guilty beyond a reasonable doubt to the above offenses. Further note that the defendant is not required to prove his innocence. Defendants are not even required to present a defense.

People of the State Illinois vs. Lyla Bloom

MISS DAISY MORALES, called as a witness, having been sworn, was examined and testified as follows:

DIRECT EXAMINATION by Mr. Weiss, prosecutor for the people of the State of Illinois: Could you state your name for the record?

Miss Morales: Luz Maria Daisy Morales.

Mr. Weiss: Where do you live?

Miss Morales: I live in Chicago. 1450 N. Paulina Street.

Mr. Weiss: How old are you?

Miss Morales: I am twenty years old.

Mr. Weiss: Do you work?

Miss Morales: Yes, I do.

Mr. Weiss: Where do you work and what do you do?

Miss Morales: I work at Goldbrick's Department Store in the deli department. It is like a restaurant section except there are no chairs. It is a stand-up, walk-up counter and we serve sandwiches, soups, and cold drinks. It is mainly fast food. But our signature product is a sandwich from our fresh deli.

Mr. Weiss: How long have you been working at the Goldbrick's Department Store?

Miss Morales: I have been working for four and a half months.

Mr. Weiss: Miss Morales, bringing your attention to July tenth, on or about 10:30 a.m., what, if anything, were you doing?

Miss Morales: Oh, I was at work. I had been at work since 8:00 a.m., when the store opens.

Mr. Weiss: What were you doing that morning?

Miss Morales: I was setting up the restaurant and taking care of the morning crowd. The morning crowd usually has an appetite for hot chocolate, or hot coffee, bagels, sweets rolls, and donuts.

Mr. Weiss: Miss Morales, drawing your attention to about 10:30 a.m., what, if anything, happened?

Miss Morales: What do you mean? Do you mean when Mrs. Bloom came in?

Ms. Sommers, defense attorney: Objection, your Honor.

The Court: The objection will be sustained.

Mr. Weiss: Miss Morales, please tell the court what happened on July tenth around 10:30 a.m.

Miss Morales: Well, at about 10:30 a.m. I was dusting off the counter tops when I saw Mrs. Bloom staring through the display windows where all the deli meats are, and the cheeses. As soon as I saw her, I asked her if I could help her out.

Mr. Weiss: Hold it, Miss Morales. This Mrs. Bloom, do you recognize that person? Is she in the courtroom?

Miss Morales: Yes, she is sitting right there, right in front of the table, right next to her lawyer.

Mr. Weiss: Miss Morales, can you identify a piece of clothing that she is wearing?

Miss Morales: It is the lady who is wearing the hat with the three feathers.

Mr. Weiss: Thank you, Miss Morales. Let the record reflect that the witness has testified and has properly identified the defendant in this case.

The Court: Thank you, counsel. The record will so reflect. You may continue.

Mr. Weiss: Miss Morales, when you asked the defendant if you could help her, what did she say?

Miss Morales: Oh, she said no. Actually, she just moved her head left to right in a 'no' fashion. I had to ask her a few times until she spoke. Our training is that we must have an audible response. She finally did say no in her soft voice, that she did not need any help, that she was just looking. But she was dragging that little shopping cart she always pulls and the day before she knocked down all of the onion buns and the Parmesan-covered bagels.

Ms. Sommers: Objection, your Honor.

The Court: Objection sustained. Attorney Weiss, please present a question.

Mr. Weiss: Miss Morales, going back to the first words that you addressed to the defendant, how are you sure that you asked if you could help her?

Miss Morales: The training that we have is we always greet the customers with "Good morning, may I help you?" And that is exactly what I asked. And she said no.

Mr. Weiss: Thank you, Miss Morales. What happened next?

Miss Morales: I continued making spotless the countertops and display windows and I guess that she—Mrs. Bloom—may have drifted into another part of the store.

Mr. Weiss: What happened next, Miss Morales?

Miss Morales: Mrs. Bloom came back, and this time I spotted her staring into the cheese and meat section of the counter. By now it's about 11:30 and it's becoming a little busy.

Mr. Weiss: Yes, Miss Morales, and what happened next?

Miss Morales: I finished my last customer, who was ordering pastrami on a kosher roll without mustard, and I saw Mrs. Bloom still staring at the meats. So I made a comment like, "Hi, you are back again," and she nodded yes. So I asked her, "Are you hungry?" and she nodded yes.

Mr. Weiss: What happened next?

Miss Morales: Then I asked her, "Would you like a sandwich?" and she said yes. So I asked her what kind of sandwich she wanted, and she just stared at me. Then she nodded yes again. So I asked her if she wanted the special. I told her the special was ham with Irish Swiss cheese, that those are pretty good. So I asked her if she would like one of those, and she said yes. Well, I asked her if she wanted it on a kosher roll. The customer has a choice of breads, you know. But she just stared at me again. I told her the sandwiches are good on a kosher roll. That's my favorite. Then she nodded yes, so I started making the sandwich special on a kosher roll. She said she wanted lettuce, tomatoes, mayonnaise; actually she wanted everything on it with an extra pickle. I gave her extra pickles. This makes the customer happier. That has been my idea.

Mr. Weiss: Miss Morales, did you proceed to prepare the sandwich as instructed by Mrs. Bloom?

Miss Morales: Yes, I did. I finished the sandwich, cut it in two, and gave the extra pickles, and then I offered her either a bag of potato chips or french fries. These items come with the special. I gave her the bag of potato chips.

Mr. Weiss: Okay, Miss Morales, what happened next?

Miss Morales: I asked her if she wanted a drink with the meal and she said yes. I offered her a soft drink or a coffee.

Mr. Weiss: What did she say to you and what did you say to her?

Miss Morales: I asked her if she wanted a soft drink or coffee, but she would not talk. I finally got her to say that she preferred the coffee, so I gave her a cup of coffee.

Mr. Weiss: So what happened next?

Miss Morales: Mrs. Bloom used about twenty napkins to wipe the lip of the coffee cup. She kept wiping and wiping, you know, wiping the germs around the edge of the coffee cup.

Mr. Weiss: What happened next?

Miss Morales: She started to act as if the coffee was too hot. I guess she wanted an ice cube in the coffee.

Mr. Weiss: What did you do next?

Miss Morales: So I put some ice cubes in the coffee cup, and I gave her the coffee. She took no sugar or cream, but she took extra napkins. She just kept polishing the rim of the coffee cup as if there was lipstick or dirt on it. She really doesn't like germs.

Mr. Weiss: What happened next, Miss Morales?

Miss Morales: She started to drink the coffee and I told her it would be $4.98, tax included.

Mr. Weiss: What happened next?

Miss Morales: She looked at me as if I was from another planet.

Ms. Sommers: Objection.

The Court: Sustained.

Mr. Weiss: Miss Morales, when you asked her to pay $4.98, what happened next?

Miss Morales: She just kept looking at me, staring at me, as if I was not talking to her and then proceeded not to give me any attention and she started to make her way out of the dining area.

Mr. Weiss: Okay, Miss Morales, when she started making her way out of the dining room she did not pay, did she?

Ms. Sommers: Objection, your Honor, this is leading.

The Court: Sustained.

Mr. Weiss: Miss Morales, did Mrs. Bloom pay for her sandwich?

Miss Morales: No, she did not. She proceeded to walk right out and was not paying any attention to my demands for payment, and that is when she bumped—she stumbled—into Mr. Hobbs.

Mr. Weiss: Miss Morales, who is Mr. Hobbs?

Miss Morales: Mr. Hobbs is the floor manager of the department store. He was on duty that day. He was probably coming in to get a sandwich himself.

Mr. Weiss: What happened next?

Miss Morales: I told... I pointed out to Mr. Hobbs that Mrs. Bloom was leaving without paying for her sandwich.

Mr. Weiss: Okay, what happened next?

Miss Morales: Well, Mrs. Bloom was told to stop and then Mr. Hobbs grabbed her. He really was grabbing at the sandwich. Mrs. Bloom would not give up her sandwich and that is when Mr. Hobbs got baptized with the coffee. It just so happened that security was coming in, probably getting a sandwich too. That is when Mr. Hobbs got Mrs. Bloom arrested. Mr. Hobbs was furious because of his coffee-stained trousers.

Mr. Weiss: Miss Morales, when security came, they arrested Mrs. Bloom for stealing?

Ms. Sommers: Objection, your Honor, the prosecution is leading.

The Court: Objection is sustained.

Mr. Weiss: Miss Morales, can you tell the court why Mrs. Bloom was arrested?

Ms. Sommers: Objection.

Mr. Weiss: Your Honor, can the court inquire as to the nature of the objection?

Ms. Sommers: We are assuming a fact not in evidence. We are assuming that Mrs. Bloom was arrested at that moment. Secondly, this witness cannot possibly know what kind of charges or even if an arrest was made. Miss Morales is an employee who makes sandwiches.

Mr. Weiss: Your Honor, I will withdraw the question. We will call security as our next witness to establish that Mrs. Bloom was in fact detained and ultimately charged after her arrest.

The Court: Very good. Any additional questions, Mr. Weiss?

Mr. Weiss: Just a few questions. Miss Morales, you were in charge of collecting money from the customer after attending to them?

Miss Morales: Yes.

Mr. Weiss: Did Mrs. Bloom pay you for the sandwich meal?

Miss Morales: No, she did not.

Mr. Weiss: No more questions for this witness.

The Court: Any questions, Ms. Sommers?

Ms. Sommers: Absolutely.

CROSS EXAMINATION by Ms. Sommers: Miss Morales, you have testified that you have been working for Goldbrick's Department Store for four and a half months. Is that true?

Miss Morales: Yes, it is, ma'am.

Ms. Sommers: Miss Morales, you were not working all four and a half months at the deli shop, were you?

Miss Morales: No, ma'am.

Ms. Sommers: As a matter of fact, Miss Morales, this was your first day selling sandwiches. Is that true?

Miss Morales: No, ma'am. Actually it was my second day at this assignment.

Ms. Sommers: Actually, Miss Morales, the first day you spent learning how to keep your workstation clean and how to deal with the clientele. Isn't that true?

Miss Morales: Yes, ma'am, I did not make any sales on my first day.

Ms. Sommers: Miss Morales, you had one day of training. Isn't that true?

Miss Morales: At the deli shop, yes, but I have been dealing with the public since I started at Goldbrick's.

Ms. Sommers: Yes, Miss Morales, but for serving sandwiches at the deli shop you were given one day's training. Is that true?

Miss Morales: Yes, ma'am.

Ms. Sommers: Going back to your dealings with the public Miss Morales, you say you have been dealing with the public for four and a half months. Is that true?

Miss Morales: Yes.

Ms. Sommers: In all the time that you worked in the different departments, did you ever see Mrs. Bloom in the different departments of the store?

Miss Morales: Yes, I have.

Ms. Sommers: Have you seen her more than one time?

Miss Morales: Yes, I have seen her a lot of times.

Ms. Sommers: More than ten times?

Miss Morales: I would say almost every day that I have been at work, I have seen Mrs. Bloom. It is usually in the morning and she is always pulling her shopping cart.

Ms. Sommers: Miss Morales, the shopping cart you are referencing is the same one she had the day of the incident?

Miss Morales: Yes, it is.

Ms. Sommers: Miss Morales, you identified Mrs. Bloom this morning when the State's attorney asked you. You identified her by her hat. Do you remember?

Miss Morales: Yes, I did.

Ms. Sommers: So you recognize Mrs. Bloom by her hat?

Miss Morales: Oh, yes, she wears the same faded hat, with the same faded pink plumage. It's always the same outfit.

Ms. Sommers: Mrs. Bloom's hat is pretty old, isn't it?

Mr. Weiss: Objection.

The Court: Objection is sustained.

Ms. Sommers: Miss Morales, those feathers in her hat look pretty stale and faded—

Mr. Weiss: Objection.

The Court: Objection sustained. Attorney Sommers, this hearing is not about Mrs. Bloom's attire. Go on to something else.

Ms. Sommers: Miss Morales, in all of your dealings with Mrs. Bloom, you have never sold her anything?

Miss Morales: No, no, Ms. Sommers, no, I have not.

Ms. Sommers: Have you ever seen her buy anything, Miss Morales?

Miss Morales: No, I have not. These old people usually don't have any money. I was even thinking of paying for the sandwich myself, but then Mr. Hobbs got there. He knew something was up because he demanded to know if there was some trouble.

Ms. Sommers: You have personally never sold Mrs. Bloom anything, have you?

Miss Morales: No, I have not.

Ms. Sommers: Miss Morales, when you first asked Mrs. Bloom if she wanted the food she did not answer. Is that true?

Miss Morales: What do you mean?

Ms. Sommers: You had to ask her a few times, right?

Miss Morales: Mrs. Bloom just stood there like in a daze.

Ms. Sommers: That's right, she doesn't talk much.

Miss Morales: But she did nod!

Ms. Sommers: Yes. She nodded yes at the sandwich that you offered. Isn't that a fact?

Miss Morales: Yes.

Ms. Sommers: And she nodded yes at the kind of sandwich you suggested?

Miss Morales: Yes.

Ms. Sommers: You also picked the kind of bread for her sandwich?

Miss Morales: Mrs. Bloom was just standing there and would not decide.

Ms. Sommers: That's right, you also picked for her the bag of potato chips and offered it to her. Isn't that a fact?

Miss Morales: Fries or chips came with the special. They had a choice.

Ms. Sommers: Yes, the customer has a choice, you said that. But you did the choosing and the offering with the bag of potato chips. And you did the choosing and the offering with the beverage. Isn't that what happened?

Miss Morales: Mrs. Bloom was so slow in deciding and I had some customers piling up.

Ms. Sommers: On the day of the incident, did you ever see Mrs. Bloom attack Mr. Hobbs?

Miss Morales: No, I have not, no, I did not. She is a real small lady.

Ms. Sommers: Did you ever see Mrs. Bloom throw coffee at Mr. Hobbs?

Miss Morales: No, I did not.

Ms. Sommers: Did you see Mrs. Bloom hit Mr. Hobbs over the head with a coffee cup?

Miss Morales: No, I did not.

Ms. Sommers: Did you see Mrs. Bloom burn Mr. Hobbs with hot coffee?

Miss Morales: Not with the coffee we sell. We don't sell the coffee that hot to begin with. Management is afraid of being sued, just like McDonald's got sued for selling hot coffee.

Ms. Sommers: Miss Morales, you put ice cubes in Mrs. Bloom's cup of coffee, didn't you?

Miss Morales: Yes, I did. It appears that Mrs. Bloom liked her coffee cooler than lukewarm.

Ms. Sommers: Well, Miss Morales, Mrs. Bloom never asked for ice cubes, did she?

Miss Morales: That is true, but she looked like she could use them ice cubes.

Ms. Sommers: You offered ice cubes for her coffee and she accepted?

Miss Morales: Yes.

Ms. Sommers: Now, Miss Morales, I would like to go over one last area with you regarding Mrs. Bloom. Was Mrs. Bloom ever confrontational with you? Did she ever yell at you or raise her voice?

Miss Morales: No, ma'am, she speaks in a very low voice like a grandma. Besides, all she mainly does is nod. She does a lot of nodding yes and no with her head. She is an older lady. You can hardly hear her anyways.

Ms. Sommers: Well, Miss Morales, when you demanded payment for the sandwich, what did she say to you?

Miss Morales: She only said that she had no money.

Ms. Sommers: Did she say anything else? That's it? That she had no money, or did you understand she had no money?

Miss Morales: Well, Ms. Sommers, Mrs. Bloom was really drinking her coffee and trying to hold her sandwich in her left hand and trying to hold a bag of potato chips and her purse while dragging a shopping cart. There was nothing in the shopping cart but a box, and the box was empty.

Ms. Sommers: Miss Morales, when Mr. Hobbs arrived at the scene, did you hear Mrs. Bloom raise her voice or say anything else?

Miss Morales: No, Mrs. Bloom did become somewhat agitated though.

Ms. Sommers: Miss Morales, did you hear her say anything to Mr. Hobbs?

Miss Morales: The only thing I heard her say was, "It is mine, mine." She may have repeated "mine" once or twice.

Ms. Sommers: When did this happen?

Miss Morales: It happened when Mr. Hobbs tried to take away her sandwich.

Mr. Weiss: Objection, hearsay! Move to strike.

Ms. Sommers: Your Honor, these communications happened within the hearing range of Miss Morales. She has personal knowledge of this conversation.

The Court: Objection overruled. Attorney Sommers, continue with your examination.

Ms. Sommers: Your Honor, this concludes the examination of Miss Morales.

The Court: Any additional questions of this witness?

Ms. Sommers: No, your Honor.

Mr. Weiss: Your Honor, the State calls Mr. Hobbs to the stand.

The Court: Okay then, Miss Morales, you are excused. Thank you for coming. You may stay in the courtroom now if you wish. The clerk will call Mr. Hobbs to the stand.

TIMOTHY HOBBS, called as a witness, having been sworn, was examined and testified as follows:

EXAMINATION by Mr. Weiss: What is your name?

Mr. Hobbs: Timothy Hobbs.

Mr. Weiss: What is your occupation?

Mr. Hobbs: I am the floor manager of Goldbrick's Department Store. I work the day shift. I was just promoted. I am in charge of all the departments during the day time.

Mr. Weiss: Mr. Hobbs, are you familiar with the defendant, Mrs. Bloom?

Mr. Hobbs: Yes, she is the woman who attacked me—

Ms. Sommers: Objection!

The Court: Objection sustained.

Mr. Weiss: On the date of the incident, were you on duty working your regular shift at Goldbrick's Department Store?

Mr. Hobbs: Yes, I was.

Mr. Weiss: On or about 11:00 or 11:30 that morning, did you have occasion to be at the deli department?

Mr. Hobbs: Yes, I did. It is my practice to take lunch about 11:15 or at least before 11:30. I get my sandwich so I can beat the rush.

Mr. Weiss: When you arrived at the deli department what, if anything, unusual happened?

Mr. Hobbs: As I walked into the deli department, I overheard Miss

Morales asking Mrs. Bloom to pay for a sandwich she was carrying.

Mr. Weiss: What, if anything, happened next?

Mr. Hobbs: I saw Mrs. Bloom making no efforts to reach for her purse or pay for the food that she had in her hands.

Mr. Weiss: Well, hold it a second, Mr. Hobbs. When you arrived at the deli, who was present?

Mr. Hobbs: There was present Miss Morales behind the counter. There were some other patrons who were being attended by some other employees. And Miss Morales was attending to three other customers who were also ordering sandwiches. We were having a special that day of honey-glazed ham with Irish Swiss cheese. It is very popular on Tuesdays, especially since we started adding potato chips and french fries and a beverage. It is an excellent idea. As a matter of fact, it was my—

Mr. Weiss: Mr. Hobbs, aside from Miss Morales and other customers, who else was present?

Mr. Hobbs: Oh, Mrs. Bloom was present and she had in her hands a cup of hot coffee, a bag of potato chips, and a ham and Swiss cheese special sandwich on the kosher roll. Mrs. Bloom was sipping on her coffee with absolutely no intention of paying for the daily special.

Ms. Sommers: Objection, move to strike.

The Court: Objection sustained. The last sentence of the response will be stricken from the record.

Mr. Weiss: Mr. Hobbs, when you first got to the deli, did you hear Miss Morales say anything to Mrs. Bloom?

Mr. Hobbs: Yes, she was asking Mrs. Bloom to pay $4.98. Mrs. Bloom was not responding or saying anything and I did not want an incident to happen, so I walked straight to Mrs. Bloom and asked her if there was anything wrong or if I could be of any assistance, as I would do with any of our valued customers.

Mr. Weiss: Mr. Hobbs, what happened next?

Mr. Hobbs: Mrs. Bloom proceeded to violently attack me. She threw the coffee at my face. My eye was almost plucked from its socket when it was hit with an ice cube. When I tried to cover myself and defend myself, she proceeded to hit me over the head with the coffee cup. For a second I thought that Mrs. Bloom had lost her mind. Here is a senior citizen acting violent, acting up like that in our fine establishment. Can you imagine? Well, I just moved back and allowed security to move in. Fortunately, security was there in a few seconds. Our security is always alert and ready to serve.

Mr. Weiss: What happened next, Mr. Hobbs?

Mr. Hobbs: Next, I stepped back and allowed security to handle an irate, bad-mouthing elderly woman. You understand that the police department had to be called to subdue her. I was very afraid. A woman who can attack me with hot coffee is also capable of hitting me with the shopping cart that she pulls along. That shopping cart is a dangerous weapon, I tell you.

Mr. Weiss: Hold it, Mr. Hobbs. There are no more questions. Judge, there are no more questions. We excuse the witness.

The Court: Attorney Sommers, do you have any questions of Mr. Hobbs?

Ms. Sommers: Yes, I do, your Honor, yes, I do, thank you.

CROSS EXAMINATION by Ms. Sommers.

Ms. Sommers: You recently mentioned, sir, that you were attacked by Mrs. Bloom with a coffee cup.

Mr. Weiss: Objection.

The Court: Sustained. Ms. Sommers, if you have a question, present the question. You may continue.

Ms. Sommers: You stated you were hit with a cup, a coffee cup, on the head. Is that true?

Mr. Hobbs: Yes, it is.

Ms. Sommers: On what part of your head were you struck with this coffee cup?

Mr. Hobbs: I was struck right about here.

Ms. Sommers: Your Honor, the record should reflect that the witness is indicating that he was struck in the face higher than the eyebrows, just below the hairline of the left side of his face.

The Court: The record will so indicate. Attorney Sommers, you may continue.

Ms Sommers: The cup you say you were hit with was a paper cup. Isn't that true?

Mr. Hobbs: I don't know what kind of cup. It was not a metal cup, that is correct.

Ms. Sommers: It was not a hard, plastic cup?

Mr. Hobbs: No, it was not.

Ms. Sommers: It was a cardboard paper cup. Isn't that true?

Mr. Hobbs: All right, I guess it was.

Ms. Sommers: That is the kind of cup you would serve coffee in. Isn't that true?

Mr. Hobbs: Yes, it is.

Ms. Sommers: Now, Mr. Hobbs, when you got hit in the forehead with this paper cup, you didn't receive any gashes, did you?

Mr. Hobbs: I am sorry. I did not understand that question.

Ms. Sommers: Your injuries did not require any stitches. That is true?

Mr. Hobbs: That is correct.

Ms. Sommers: There wasn't any bleeding because of your injury, was there, Mr. Hobbs?

Mr. Hobbs: No, there was no bleeding, but she tried to burn my face.

Ms. Sommers: Hold off, Mr. Hobbs, we will get to the liquids in a second, but the injuries you sustained on your forehead did not require medical attention. Is that true?

Mr. Hobbs: Well, I got hit in the face pretty hard, and she tried to burn me with the hot coffee.

Ms. Sommers: Mr. Hobbs, you did not go to the hospital after the injury, did you?

Mr. Hobbs: No, I did not.

Ms. Sommers: You did not go to the doctor after the injury. Isn't that true?

Mr. Hobbs: Yes, that is true.

Ms. Sommers: The ambulance was not called after this injury. Isn't that true?

Mr. Hobbs: I called the police.

Ms. Sommers: Your Honor, can you please instruct the witness to just answer the questions that I am presenting? Thank you, Judge.

The Court: Mr. Hobbs, the answers you are giving are not answers to the questions as presented by Ms. Sommers. Please listen carefully to the questions, and just answer that question. Thank you.

Ms. Sommers: Did you have to call the ambulance?

Mr. Hobbs: No, the ambulance was not called.

Ms. Sommers: Mr. Hobbs, you did not receive a bruise from your attack on the forehead, did you?

Mr. Hobbs: That is true.

Ms. Sommers: You did not have any red marks on your forehead. Isn't that true?

Mr. Hobbs: That is true.

Ms. Sommers: That is because you were not hit in the face. Isn't that true?

Mr. Weiss: Objection, your Honor.

Ms. Sommers: I will ask a different question, Judge.

The Court: Continue, Ms. Sommers.

Ms. Sommers: Mr. Hobbs, when you were hit in the face with the coffee cup, you did not sustain any burns on your face from the liquid. Isn't that true?

Mr. Hobbs: I got soaked.

Ms. Sommers: Excuse me, Mr. Hobbs. Your face was not burned, was it?

Mr. Hobbs: That is correct. No, I did not really receive any burns.

Ms. Sommers: That's because when you got hit in the head the cup was empty. Isn't that true?

Mr. Hobbs: I was soaking wet!

Ms. Sommers: If you had been burned, you would have gone to the hospital. Isn't that true?

Mr. Weiss: Objection.

The Court: Sustained.

Ms. Sommers: You did state, Mr. Hobbs, that you were hit in the eye with an ice cube.

Mr. Hobbs: I was *spit* in the eye. She spit an ice cube in my eye.

Ms. Sommers: That was right after you made Mrs. Bloom spill her coffee?

Mr. Weiss: Objection.

The Court: Sustained.

Ms. Sommers: Mr. Hobbs, you were real close to Mrs. Bloom when you got spit in the eye, weren't you?

Mr. Hobbs: We were pretty close.

Ms. Sommers: How far away from her were you?

Mr. Hobbs: I don't remember. Not too far.

Ms. Sommers: You were pretty close. You were in her face, weren't you?

Mr. Hobbs: No, I was just close to her, about one or two feet away.

Ms. Sommers: You would say you were an arm's length away from her?

Mr. Hobbs: About that distance.

Ms. Sommers: That is when you tried to take her sandwich away?

Mr. Hobbs: Yes, that sandwich did not belong to her.

Ms. Sommers: But Mr. Hobbs, you were hit in the face with the ice cube when you tried to take the sandwich away. Isn't that correct?

Mr. Hobbs: Somehow she hit me with the ice cube real hard in the eye.

Ms. Sommers: Yeah, practically knocked your eyeball right out of your socket.

Mr. Weiss: Objection!

Ms. Sommers: Judge, that is what he testified to. "Practically plucked out of its socket." That's what he said.

The Court: That is enough, Ms. Sommers. Go on to something else.

Ms. Sommers: You say that Mrs. Bloom hit you on the head with the cup. Is that true?

Mr. Hobbs: Yes, it is.

Ms. Sommers: And this is also the time that she tried to burn your hands and your face. Isn't that right?

Mr. Hobbs: Yes, it is.

Ms. Sommers: Would you say you were struggling at the time with Mrs. Bloom?

Mr. Hobbs: Yes, I would say that she was being resistant.

Ms. Sommers: Yes, Mr. Hobbs, you were trying to stop her from leaving?

Mr. Hobbs: Not really trying to stop her, but she was not going anywhere, that is correct.

Ms. Sommers: You and Mrs. Bloom were just struggling or wrestling over the sandwich. That is what happened. Isn't that true?

Mr. Hobbs: I was just trying to prevent a crime from being committed in my presence.

Ms. Sommers: But you were not trying to stop Mrs. Bloom. You were trying to take away her sandwich. Isn't that true?

Mr. Hobbs: Yes, that is true, but I was also trying to hold her for security to arrive.

Ms. Sommers: Okay, Mr. Hobbs, when did you call security?

Mr. Hobbs: What do you mean, Ms. Sommers?

Ms. Sommers: Mr. Hobbs, isn't it a fact that you did not call security?

Mr. Hobbs: Oh, security did come. They came right away.

Ms. Sommers: Mr. Hobbs, you did not call security. Isn't that true, isn't that a fact?

Mr. Hobbs: That's correct, I did not call security.

Ms. Sommers: As a matter of fact, you don't know how security got there, do you?

Mr. Hobbs: Well, they showed up right away.

Ms. Sommers: Yes, Mr. Hobbs, but you did not call them?

Mr. Hobbs: That is true.

Ms. Sommers: You did not call the police either, did you?

Mr. Hobbs: No, I did not call the police.

Ms. Sommers: You did not call for help, did you, Mr. Hobbs?

Mr. Hobbs: No, I did not.

Ms. Sommers: A big guy like you, Mr. Hobbs, does not need any help wrestling an old lady, do you?

Mr. Weiss: Objection.

The Court: Sustained.

Ms. Sommers: Mr. Hobbs, isn't it true that you don't like old people?

Mr. Weiss: Objection.

The Court: Sustained.

Ms. Sommers: Mr. Hobbs, during that time there was an influx of senior citizens coming into the store. Isn't that true?

Mr. Hobbs: Yes, there had been an increase of movement of older people.

Ms. Sommers: That is because the McDonald's down the block had stopped allowing the senior citizens to congregate for their morning coffees at the McDonald's. Isn't that right?

Mr. Weiss: Objection.

The Court: The objection is overruled. You may answer, Mr. Hobbs, if you know.

Mr. Hobbs: The senior citizens were taking up too much space over at the McDonald's. They would buy a cup of coffee at 7:00 a.m. and stay til noon occupying the booths. There was no place for the paying customers to sit. It was getting real bad. It was like a senior citizen convention. When the old people got kicked out of McDonald's in the mornings, they decided to just stroll and spend their time in my store.

Ms. Sommers: Mr. Hobbs, the old people, they don't spend much money, do they?

Mr. Hobbs: No, they don't. They are on a limited income. All they do is buy a cup of coffee and nurse that cup all morning.

Ms. Sommers: Yes, but in your store, the seniors as a group do not buy much, do they?

Mr. Hobbs: No, they don't. They just walk in and window shop.

Ms. Sommers: As a matter of fact, you took away all the benches and chairs so that there would be no loitering inside the department store. Is that true?

Mr. Hobbs: I took the benches out, but not for those reasons. I run a store, and people are supposed to come in to buy, not socialize.

Ms. Sommers: Have the morning sales of your store been affected?

Mr. Hobbs: Yes, they have. Morning sales are soft.

Ms. Sommers: Mr. Hobbs, would you say that the decline in sales is attributed to the influx of the old people?

Mr. Hobbs: It could be, yes, it could be the old people. And it could be the economy. It could be the unemployment rate. I think I know where you are going, counselor.

Ms. Sommers: Would it be fair to say, Mr. Hobbs, there is no exact science from which you can base a reason for the decline in your store sales?

Mr. Hobbs: That is correct, but the sales, we measure them in morning, midday, and evening. And the mornings, they are way down and it's because the old people are coming in and spooking away the clientele.

Ms. Sommers: Spooking? Can you explain spooking to the court?

Mr. Hobbs: Well, it is just that they are in the way, and they don't buy. Some don't even have any money.

Ms. Sommers: Mr. Hobbs, are you telling the court that Mrs. Bloom was in your store to drive away your clients, your customers?

Mr. Hobbs: Mrs. Bloom was there every day along with her buddies. They stopped congregating at McDonald's and started walking around in the store. They are not shopping, they are socializing.

Ms. Sommers: Mr. Hobbs, you wanted to stop that practice, didn't you?

Mr. Hobbs: What do you mean, Ms. Sommers?

Ms. Sommers: You want to make an example of Mrs. Bloom by having her arrested.

Mr. Weiss: Objection.

The Court: Ms. Sommers, where are you going with this line of questioning?

Ms. Sommers: Judge, I am just trying to establish there is a motive and reason behind the singling out of Mrs. Bloom for prosecution. He is singling out old people in order to create an atmosphere of fear. He just wanted to show the rest of the gray crowd how unpleasant it would get for their group. His interest is in sending out a message, using Mrs. Bloom as an example.

Mr. Weiss: Judge, Mr. Hobbs is not on trial here. Mrs. Bloom is on trial for theft. Ms. Sommers seems to forget this.

The Court: Objection overruled. You many continue, Attorney Sommers. Please make your connections and make your points. Tie this in somehow.

Ms. Sommers: Mr. Hobbs, you have given instructions to your staff to be extra alert regarding old people congregating inside the store. Isn't that true?

Mr. Hobbs: I did not tell anybody to keep old people out of the store.

Ms. Sommers: You brought to the attention of your store employees that old people, or a wave of senior citizens, would be coming through the store, didn't you?

Mr. Hobbs: I may have made some comments in one of our morning pep rallies.

Ms. Sommers: Yes, Mr. Hobbs, you were putting your staff on notice that the seniors were no longer welcome at McDonald's and they would be coming to your store in the mornings. You were prepping your employees, weren't you?

Mr. Hobbs: No, I was just making comments about what is common knowledge.

Ms. Sommers: You were singling out the senior citizen because they were singling out your store. Isn't that a fact?

Mr. Weiss: Objection.

The Court: Overruled. You may continue, Ms. Sommers. I want to know what the problem is with the senior citizens.

Ms. Sommers: The bottom line is, Mr. Hobbs, that you did not want old people in your store in the morning, did you?

Mr. Weiss: Objection.

The Court: Overruled.

Ms. Sommers: Isn't it true that you implemented new rules so that the seniors would have to meet elsewhere in the morning?

Mr. Hobbs: There were no new rules. These people come for coffee first thing in the morning. They buy a cup of coffee and they nurse the coffee until 9:30 or 10:00 a.m. Then they go to a social service agency that has programs for senior citizens. You don't understand, they just loiter for hours.

Ms. Sommers: Oh, that is correct, Mr. Hobbs. You wanted them to go some place else. You wanted to make a statement with the gray crowd.

Mr. Hobbs: No, that is not true.

Ms. Sommers: You wanted the seniors to go elsewhere, right? This is the message you wanted to send to the whole group of seniors, and that is why you wanted them arrested. Isn't that correct?

Mr. Hobbs: No, that is not the case. I had her arrested because she broke the law.

Ms. Sommers: You wanted her arrested and prosecuted to the fullest extent of the law. Is that the message?

Mr. Hobbs: No, I am having her prosecuted because she broke the law.

Mr. Weiss: Objection, your Honor, badgering the witness.

Ms. Sommers: There will be no further questions.

Mr. Weiss: The State calls Mr. Charlie Base.

CHARLES BASE, called as a witness, having been sworn, was examined and testified as follows:

DIRECT EXAMINATION by Mr. Weiss: Mr. Base, state your name and occupation.

Mr. Base: My name is Charlie Base, and I work as a security guard at Goldbrick's Department Store.

Mr. Weiss: Sir, how long have been working as security?

Mr. Base: Approximately six years this coming summer.

Mr. Weiss: Bringing your attention to July tenth at around 11:00 a.m., what, if anything, happened?

Mr. Base: Well, the day started out uneventful. About 11:00 a.m. I was walking toward the deli that is in the restaurant section of the department store. This is my routine. I usually make my morning rounds. And at about 11:00 a.m. is when I grab a coffee or something to eat.

Mr. Weiss: About 11:00 a.m. what, if anything, unusual happened?

Mr. Base: I noted that Mr. Hobbs was having difficulties with the defendant, Mrs. Bloom.

Mr. Weiss: Do you see, Mrs. Bloom, the defendant, in the courtroom?

Mr. Base: Yes, she is sitting over with the defense counsel, Ms. Sommers.

Mr. Weiss: Can you identify a piece of clothing?

Mr. Base: She is the one with the hat on with the faded pink feathers.

Mr. Weiss: Judge, let the record reflect that the defendant has been identified in open court.

The Court: The record will so reflect. You may continue, Mr. Weiss.

Mr. Weiss: Once you approached Mr. Hobbs, what, if anything, did you do?

Mr. Base: The first thing I did was try to separate them, and I tried to stabilize the situation.

Mr. Weiss: What happened next?

Mr. Base: There was some yelling and pulling and pushing. So the first thing I did was try to restore order.

Mr. Weiss: What was going on at that moment?

Mr. Base: Mr. Hobbs was yelling about having been assaulted with possible lesions and burns to his face and body, showing me his wet pants. Miss Morales was saying that Mrs. Bloom was trying to leave the premises without paying for a sandwich, and Mr. Hobbs was trying to prevent Mrs. Bloom from leaving. Mr. Hobbs then instructed me to call the police.

Mr. Weiss: What, if anything, did you do then?

Mr. Base: After I assessed the situation as being stable, I proceeded to escort Mrs. Bloom to my security station, which is my office.

Mr. Weiss: What did you do next?

Mr. Base: I was instructed to call the police, and I immediately complied.

Mr. Weiss: What happened next?

Mr. Base: The Chicago Police Department came, and we wrote out a complaint charging Mrs. Bloom with retail theft and aggravated assault on a Goldbrick's Department Store employee. I then informed Mrs. Bloom of the charges, which we were proceeding to press, and asked if she wanted to sign the statement of charges, which is our custom, but she said nothing and did nothing.

Mr. Weiss: How long would you say she was in your security station while you questioned her and prepared these statements?

Mr. Base: Oh, I would say fifteen to twenty minutes.

Mr. Weiss: Okay, what happened next?

Mr. Base: By then the police arrived and we informed the police why we were detaining Mrs. Bloom, at which time she was placed in custody with the Chicago Police Department.

Mr. Weiss: In your normal course of business as security, what did you do next?

Mr. Base: I inventoried the evidence, in this case, the coffee cup and a bag of potato chips. I usually take photos of the merchandise in case the police department inventories the items for evidence. In this case, no merchandise was confiscated. And finally I put everything in a written report, which is the custom as with all other individuals who are charged by the department store, a charge meaning that the department store is going to press a complaint.

Mr. Weiss: Thank you, Mr. Base, no more questions.

The Court: Any questions, Ms. Sommers?

Ms. Sommers: Yes.

CROSS EXAMINATION by Ms. Sommers: When you took Mrs. Bloom into custody, you inventoried the evidence and you took a snapshot, is that true?

Mr. Base: Yes.

Ms. Sommers: You did not inventory the sandwich, did you?

Mr. Base: No, we did not.

Ms. Sommers: Is that because Mrs. Bloom still had the sandwich in her hands?

Mr. Base: That is correct. Mr. Hobbs was never able to take the sandwich away from Mrs. Bloom.

Ms. Sommers: Did you ever make an effort to take the sandwich for inventory purposes?

Mr. Base: Yes, I did.

Ms. Sommers: You were not successful, I gather?

Mr. Base: That is correct. She was holding that sandwich to her chest. She would not let go.

Ms. Sommers: Thank you, Mr. Base. Can you show the judge how she was holding it?

Mr. Base: Yes, she was holding it to her chest like a teddy bear. She would also say "mine." That was the word she kept repeating any time anyone got close to that sandwich.

Ms. Sommers: Were the police able to separate her from the sandwich?

Mr. Base: Not to my knowledge. When they took her to the station for processing, Mrs. Bloom left with the sandwich.

Ms. Sommers: Mr. Base, going back to when you arrived, when you first arrived at the deli, you said you assessed the situation?

Mr. Base: Yes.

Ms. Sommers: During your assessment, was there a robbery going on?

Mr. Weiss: Objection, your Honor.

The Court: Sustained.

Ms. Sommers: Mr. Base, in the assessment you made, did you note the situation to be dangerous?

Mr. Base: No, I did not.

Ms. Sommers: Did you have to call backup?

Mr. Base: No, I did not.

Ms. Sommers: How many other security members do you have?

Mr. Base: In all shifts there are four security personnel at all times. Our code name is "plumbers" so that if there is an emergency in the restaurant, the intercom will say "plumbers to the restaurant section," or "plumbers to the cosmetic department," and that is our code for security to attend to that department.

Ms. Sommers: Mr. Base, in this situation, was any backup called?

Mr. Base: I saw the situation as something I could handle without backup.

Ms. Sommers: Thank you, Mr. Base. You have seen Mrs.—strike that. You were able to identify Mrs. Bloom. Is that because you have seen her in the past?

Mr. Base: Yes, I see her every day that I come to work. I usually see her in the mornings. She comes in with the other senior citizens. It is like a morning stroll through the department store. They usually don't buy anything, and they are pretty harmless. They just walk around for awhile and then they are gone. They don't cause any trouble. And Mrs. Bloom, she has never caused any trouble, to my knowledge. I never seen her buy anything either.

Ms. Sommers: When you escorted Mrs. Bloom to your security office, did you handcuff Mrs. Bloom?

Mr. Base: No, I did not.

Ms. Sommers: Did she go peacefully with you?

Mr. Base: Yes, she did. She seemed relieved that we were going away from the area of the disturbance.

Ms. Sommers: You mean she was calming down because she was going away from Mr. Hobbs?

Mr. Base: Well, that is one of the reasons for sure.

Ms. Sommers: When she went to your office, she was peaceful and cooperative?

Mr. Base: She was peaceful and cooperative for a while. Then, when she was not allowed to leave, she became agitated.

Ms. Sommers: That was during the time that she tried to retrieve her coffee cup and her potato chips?

Mr. Weiss: Objection.

The Court: Overruled, you may respond.

Mr. Base: Yes, she wanted her potato chips for sure. And to be frank, she was expecting another cup of coffee.

Ms. Sommers: How was that, Mr. Base?

Mr. Base: Well, she was claiming that Mr. Hobbs had spilled her coffee. She wanted her cup refilled, no cream, no sugar, just lots of napkins. She was trying to explain that her cup was not clean.

Ms. Sommers: Mr. Base, I show you defense exhibit number fifteen: do you recognize this item?

Mr. Base: Yes, this is a photo taken of Mr. Hobbs immediately after the incident. I took the photo myself.

Ms. Sommers: Bringing your attention to Mr. Hobbs' shirt, is it clean?

Mr. Base: I'm sorry?

Ms. Sommers: There is no blood or coffee stain on it. Is that correct?

Mr. Base: Yes, correct.

Ms. Sommers: The only part of Mr. Hobb's clothes that appear wet are his trousers, correct?

Mr. Base: Yes, his left leg got some coffee spill.

Ms. Sommers: The wet leg is consistent with struggling to get out of the way as opposed to an attack.

Mr. Weiss: Objection, Judge. This witness can't testify as to how this happened.

Ms. Sommers: Judge, this man is head of security. At minimum he's qualified to testify if this coffee was spilled on or thrown at Mr. Hobbs.

The Court: Objection, overruled. Mr. Base, tell us what you know.

Mr. Base: It appears the spillage on the leg is consistent with someone bumping into a cup of coffee as opposed to the coffee being flung as an attack. The coffee would have covered a wider range of space if it had been thrown at Mr. Hobbs.

Ms. Sommers: Mr. Base, do you consider your report to be thorough?

Mr. Base: Yes, I do.

Ms. Sommers: As a matter of fact, you have been on the job almost six years, and you have written many reports, correct?

Mr. Base: That is true.

Ms. Sommers: In the reports that you made for this incident, you would have covered in the form of a narrative, everything that happened, plus taken photos?

Mr. Base: That is correct.

Ms. Sommers: In your report, sir, did you note any incident on any of the parties that would have required medical attention?

Mr. Base: That is a negative.

Ms. Sommers: Did you report any parties needing medical attention?

Mr. Base: No, if there were, I would have written it down.

Ms. Sommers: If there were a need to call an ambulance, would it have been reflected in your notes?

Mr. Base: That is true and I would have taken an extra photo too.

Ms. Sommers: If you had noted a trauma to someone's face or head, that is a fact you would have noted in your reports?

Mr. Base: That is true.

Ms. Sommers: Did you see anybody get burned?

Mr. Base: No, I did not.

Ms. Sommers: If somebody would have been burned or hurt in the face, let's say Mr. Hobbs or another employee, you would have noted that in your report?

Mr. Base: That is correct. It is our policy also to call and report that to the police and we will request an ambulance to be present. It is for insurance purposes, you know.

Ms. Sommers: Mr. Base, isn't it a fact that you offered to pay for the sandwich on behalf of Mrs. Bloom?

Mr. Weiss: Objection, your Honor.

The Court: Sustained. Attorney Sommers, where are you going?

Ms. Sommers: I will ask a different question, Judge. Mr. Base, did you press or recommend charges against Mrs. Bloom with the Chicago Police Department?

Mr. Base: No, I did not. Mr. Hobbs did that. He is the floor manager.

Ms. Sommers: Have you ever pressed charges against any person for stealing a sandwich?

Mr. Weiss: Objection, your Honor, a theft is a theft, whether it is a sandwich or a TV set. It is still stealing.

Ms. Sommers: Judge, all of this food was offered to Mrs. Bloom, and Mr. Hobbs knows it. They gave a present to this lady. The whole store knew she didn't have any money. Judge, I will withdraw the questions.

Ms. Sommers: Sir, Mrs. Bloom walks real slowly, doesn't she?

Mr. Base: Yes, she does, she takes baby steps. When she pulls that cart, she does not walk fast.

Ms. Sommers: When you were assessing the situation, Mr. Base, you were told that Mrs. Bloom had not made payment for the food items, and Mr. Hobbs would like to retrieve these goods. Is that right?

Mr. Base: Yes.

Ms. Sommers: And what did Mrs. Bloom tell you?

Mr. Base: She said the nice girl, meaning Miss Morales, gave her the sandwich, and that the sandwich was "mine."

Ms. Sommers: Is that when you offered to pay for the sandwich?

Mr. Weiss: Objection.

The Court: Will both attorneys approach the bench? We will conclude testimony for the day. We will now go off the record.

This was all the testimony of value that was taken that day. Based on the above facts, evidence, and testimony presented, what would your verdict be as to the:

Crime of theft: _____guilty_____not guilty

Crime of assault: _____guilty_____ not guilty

Crime of Battery_____guilty_____ not guilty

QUESTIONS FOR THE READER

1. In *The Telegram Man,* do you agree with Reverend McCarthy's assessment of what happens in the United States to newly arrived immigrants?

2. What kind of "business" do you think Mrs. Winfield was in?

3. Would you consider Mrs. Winfield: a) a lunatic? b) highly educated? c) a gifted person? d) a murderer with weird behavior? e) a victim of false accusation?

4. *Obsessed With The Obvious* states that, "A crime committed because of a passion for a cause is not to be confused with a crime of passion." What do you think of Ortiz's assessment of the criminal mind and the crime that is committed?

5. The author plays with human prejudices to show how what may look obvious is not obvious. In *Obsessed With The Obvious,* how is Stefanski's judgment clouded by his bigotry as it pertains to the Puerto Rican detective?

6. What does "Renaissance" mean?

7. How is the philosopher Aristotle associated with the term Renaissance?

8. The term "grace" has numerous definitions and can be used as a noun and verb. In what ways is the term "grace" intertwined in the story *Saving Grace*? What is Sister Grace

trying to save?

9. What is the "gift of discernment" that Sister Grace claims to have?

10. Does Willie Stone's soul go to heaven or to hell? Based on your answer, is Sister Grace doing good or evil?

11. What is a protagonist? What is an antagonist? Which one is Sister Grace?

12. How is the title of *A Debt Collected* connected to the story?

13. In this story, how was Luigi planning on outwitting the Devil?

14. Do you think Luigi is worthy of a defense?

15. What kind of battle occurred at Tita's house? Against what forces?

16. What are considered the Seven Deadly Sins?

17. How does the author suggest that the reverend in *A Battle at Tita's House* is a proud person?

18. Both Madama and the reverend are punished for their sins. What punishment did they receive? Does the punishments fit the crime or are the punishments themselves in excess?

19. In *The Five Gold Krugerrands*, what do you think the gold coins represent to Kenny? What kind of satisfaction or joy did the coins bring him?

20. Do you think Kenny's father would have approved of the way Kenny spent his coins?

21. How does the author try to show the readers that Kenny is an educated person?

22. Are the Salvation Army impersonators justified in what they are doing? Consider that there is a "necessity defense" used in our legal system.

23. Ultimately, the coins belong to whom? How would you spend the coins?

24. Does "man just exist," as Kenny says, or does man exist for a purpose?

25. Describe the relationship of the grandmother and the grandson in *Dinner With Grandma*.

26. What changed the grandmother's mind about going out with her grandson?

27. In *State vs. Bloom*, there is an objection by Mr. Weiss based on hearsay. Do you know what hearsay is? Was the court ruling correct?

28. Do you agree with the way Mr. Hobbs was treating the senior citizens?

29. What suggestions would you give him on how to treat the senior citizens?

ABOUT THE AUTHOR

David Delgado served for many years as a judge in the Domestic
Relations Division, Circuit Court of Cook County. He is a graduate of
Wells High School in Chicago. He received his B.A. from the
University of Puerto Rico and studied law at Northwestern University
in Chicago. He taught "Trial Practice" at Chicago State University and
frequently spoke on creative writing. He is retired and lives in Chicago.

Made in the USA
Las Vegas, NV
11 January 2022

41095553R00075